Brother

by
Anita Twitchell

Edited by
Jessica Augustsson

Published by JayHenge Publishing KB

Table of Contents

CHAPTER 1

Nick scooted along the crude backless bench, as far from his stupid thirteen-year-old brother as he could. He leaned with his elbows on the rough plank table and intently searched his father's closed face.

"Please, Pa," he said. "I can cut posts as good as Sylvester can. Let me go with you today instead of him."

Mr. Wilson, seated beside his wife on an identical bench across the breakfast table, set his mouth into a stern, straight line beneath his stern straight eyebrows. It seemed to Nick that he never smiled any more.

"Don't put your elbows on the table," he said. "Bishop Taylor expects us to cut fifty cedar posts for him today. You know that Sylvester can cut posts faster than you can. We need the two quarts of grain he pays for every fifty posts we cut if we are going to get by next winter. I don't know how he kept the grasshoppers from eating all his grain but since he did, I intend to get all the grain he can spare. We are fortunate to have saved the garden. Your job is to weed it, and to look after the sheep."

Sylvester was only one year older than Nick but he was already as tall as Pa. "I told you so," he said.

Nick gagged on a spoonful of the 'lumpy dick' from his blue speckled enamel bowl. He hated the thick gooey mess his mother made from coarse-milled flour and dropped by the spoonful into the watery boiling milk. Ma said they were lucky to have it. The cow that pulled the plow and cart didn't give much milk.

"Oh please, Pa," Nick begged. "Let me go today. I hate to work alone all the time."

"You will do what you are told. You watch those sheep. If you hadn't sneaked off to that covered wagon down by the creek last spring when you should have been weeding the garden, you wouldn't be working alone now." Pa turned his face away from Nick and plunged his spoon into his bowl. He filled his mouth with lumpy dick. The discussion was over.

Heat from Nick's ears spread to burn in his cheeks. He shoved away his bowl, nearly upsetting it, and knocked over the bench, Sylvester and all, in his haste to leave the table. With a vengeance, he grabbed the covered tin bucket that held one coarse dry biscuit. He wasn't dumb enough to leave the house without his lunch. Once outside the two-room shanty that was his home, he ran and stumbled toward the sheep pen. The loose sole of his right shoe dragged and flapped in the dirt as he ran.

"I hate him! I hate him and his damned smug face," Nick said out loud. "Pa always picks him over me. Just because he is taller, Pa doesn't think Sylvester ever does anything wrong."

August that year of 1857 was a scorcher. By mid-afternoon Nick was hot, bored and lonesome. Dust swirled powdery white along the trail. Watery looking splotches shimmered ahead of him to disappear in the hot dry air. The sheep wandered toward the creek. Sweat trickled down Nick's backbone from his hair to the rawhide string he had knotted about his waist to hold the buckskin pouch that kept his most precious possessions.

He hitched Sylvester's britches a little higher. They dragged the dirt with every step. He wanted to cut them off but Ma said, "Roll them up. You're going to grow."

The rock Nick kicked along with his good left shoe, bounced toward the willows. Kick, slap. Kick, slap. Pa was going to nail that loose sole back on when he got time. Kick, slap. Kick, slap.

As he followed the sheep, Nick brooded on the conversation of the morning. Pa was right. If he and Pandy had weeded the garden like Pa'd said, everything would still be all right. Pandy wouldn't be dead now and he wouldn't be working alone. But they'd only been playing a game.

He and Pandy had just been shooting rabbits in the garden with

6

the bows and arrows Pandy's pa had made them, when Nick saw the covered wagon. Nick knew Pa had said something about a wagon as they'd eaten breakfast that early spring morning. Nick couldn't remember Pa's exact words, but he thought it was something about a boy who was staying in the wagon with his folks.

"Let's go kill the white man," Nick had told Pandy in Goshutes, the language of Pandy and his parents, the language the boys used when they played together. They crept stealthily to the canvas-covered wagon. Nick, a feather stuck in his hair, knocked on the wagon box, then climbed inside, followed by Pandy. There lay a boy with the reddest eyes and the reddest face Nick had ever seen.

"I'm Nick Wilson," Nick said. He seated himself on a wooden box near the boy's bed, while Pandy squatted on his heels next to him. "I live in the shanty by the hill." He playfully tugged Pandy's fat black braid. "This is my friend, Pandy. He is a Goshutes Indian and he can't talk much English. His pa works for my pa, and Pandy helps me."

"I'm Ethan Wells," the boy told Nick. "I have the measles. We are going to California but we had to drop out of the wagon train when I got sick."

It was a couple of weeks before Nick started to sniffle and feel headachy. He couldn't recall much after that for a while, except that he felt awfully sick. When he started getting better, Ma and Pa told him that Pandy had got the measles and died. Then in a week or so, his own baby sister got sick and died too. He wished he had never seen that wagon. Nick wished he had died instead of them. A lump rose in his throat and the salty sweat burned his eyes something fierce. He missed Pandy sorely. His ragged shirt glued itself to his back and Nick decided that Grantsville in the Utah territory was the worst place in the whole world.

Suddenly, Nick felt goose bumps tighten the skin on his arms and a shiver crawled down his back in spite of the heat. He knew he wasn't alone. He smelled them before he saw them. That smoky,

7

pungent odor could only be Indians. Pandy's parents' tepee smelled that way. Yes, there they were on the far side of the willow bunch. Three Indian men and one squaw with a couple of kids, a boy and girl about his size.

They were resting their horses—lots of horses. Some of the horses had pad saddles for riding and some of them were piled high with animal skins. The men walked up and down to stretch their legs and talked among themselves. The woman and children checked the horses, making sure all had water and the packs were secure. They were wild Indians, Nick could tell. They all wore clothes made of buckskin, not homespun pants and shirts like Pandy's ma and pa did.

I've got to get these sheep out of here before they get stolen. Quietly, he tried to head the wayward sheep back up the trail. But the sheep smelled water and they were thirsty. They refused to be driven away from it. Frustration and fear overcame Nick's caution. "Get going!" he screamed at them. With one leap a lithe, semi-nude man grabbed Nick by the arm.

"What want?" the man demanded. His voice was almost a grunt.

"Let me go!" Nick pulled hard but his arm was locked in the man's powerful grip. Panic swelled inside Nick and in desperation he kicked the Indian sharply on the shin with his good left shoe.

"Ow-wee!" The Indian hopped on one foot and rubbed his leg with his free hand. All the while, he hung on to Nick with the other. "This young cub wants to fight," he said to his companions in his own tongue. Nick was surprised. He understood every word the Indian said. Nick knew that these Indians weren't Goshutes. Goshutes Indians didn't ride horses—they ate them. They ate everything. But whoever these people were, he could understand them. Maybe they would understand him.

"Let me go," Nick said again, this time in the Goshutes language he had learned from Pandy.

"Let him go," the tallest Indian, who seemed to be the leader, said in his own language. The man who was holding Nick

8

immediately turned him loose.

When he saw that they weren't going to hurt him, Nick's fear turned to anger. "What are you doing here?" he demanded in Goshutes. "This is our land!"

The leader ignored Nick's hostility. "We go to white man city by lake of salt. We rendezvous there." He spoke broken English to Nick. "We go pronto."

"Not yet," Nick said in Goshutes. He didn't want them to leave now. He had never had an occasion to talk to a wild Indian before. If they weren't going to hurt him they might as well stay a while. Besides, he was afraid that when they went, they might take the sheep with them. If they decided that they wanted the sheep there was no way he could stop them from taking them.

So he talked to the leader while the rest of the males squatted on their heels in the shade, and the woman and girl sat cross-legged nearby. The girl giggled and covered her face with her hands whenever Nick looked at her.

"Will there be many white people at the rendezvous?" Nick asked. Again he spoke in the Indian tongue he knew.

"A great many people will be there," the leader answered Nick, abandoning his attempt at English. "Real people and men from other Indian nations come to meet with the white man to trade for things of value. We need metal arrowheads, long knives, and red blankets. Sometimes we get other things: cooking pots, coffee, too. The white man makes many useful things for us. We trade him good furs and buffalo robes when we have too many to use."

All his life, Nick had heard about the gullible Indians who came in caravans to trade precious furs for cheap glass beads and looking glasses. The traders thought it great fun to take advantage of the "heathens". Now Nick realized that the Indians felt they were getting the best of the deal, and that the white men were the stupid ones.

"The rendezvous is not far from here. Will you go?" the tall man asked Nick.

9

"I have to watch these stupid sheep," Nick said. He waved in the direction of the resting flock.

"Girl's work," the man snorted contemptuously. The girl giggled and covered her face, peeking between her fingers at Nick.

Nick glanced at her and changed the subject. "This is a nice horse," he said. He rubbed the nose of a small pinto mare. She was mostly white but large rusty brown patches, the color of Indian tobacco, splotched her hide. The horse accepted Nick's gentle touch with grateful resignation as she stood there beneath a load of buffalo skins.

"Do you want to ride this horse?" asked the tall man.

Nick nodded eagerly. The Indian boosted Nick lightly atop the load of buffalo hides. Patiently, he led the pony up the and back again, with Nick perched on top, hanging on with both hands. Nick had never been on a horse before in his entire life, not even a plow horse. He quivered with fear and delight. It was the most fun he'd had since he and Pandy had tried to ride Old Carney, the big buck sheep, last summer. Nick had pretended to be an Indian chief with a pony that ran like the wind. But Old Carney didn't like that game. He wouldn't run at all—he just laid down. Now here he was on a real Indian pony. Although he wasn't riding like the wind, or even guiding his own horse, he felt as if his dream had come true. Nick was sorry when the Indians mounted up, took their packhorses and rode off toward Great Salt Lake City.

They hadn't paid any attention to the sheep, but he sure had fun. Nick figured Sylvester would never believe him when he told his brother the tale. No white kid Nick knew had a horse. Not even Pa had a horse of his own.

"Ma, do you know what happened today?" Nick asked, after he had driven the sheep to their pen.

"Not now, Nick," his mother said. "Your pa expects to find the corn weeded when he gets home. You had better get right to it." She pushed a lock of hair from her damp forehead and sloshed Pa's other pair of britches in the old tin tub. Ma didn't like to wash clothes in the house. It made everything too hot and steamy. So she worked outside with the afternoon sun beating down on her head. "Put another piece of sagebrush on the fire and run along."

Nick tossed a gnarled grey length of the dirty brush that passed for wood onto the smoking ashes beneath the black kettle of boiling lye water and clothes in the yard. Reluctantly, he took the bow and arrows Pandy's pa had made him last year and went to the garden to pull the endless weeds and hope for a rabbit to show up. He and Pandy had become quite skilled with their bows. They had thinned out the jackrabbits considerably. Today, Nick didn't see a single one. There would be no meat for supper tonight.

"I bet you don't know what I did today," said a still-eager Nick at the supper table that evening. He had waited impatiently for Pa to finish his long-winded blessing over the food before bringing up his day's adventure.

Mr. Wilson lifted the soggy boiled pigweed greens from the bowl to his plate and doused them with vinegar. At least there were sweet baby carrots mixed with them today.

"I know what you didn't do," Mr. Wilson said, frowning. "You didn't fasten the gate to the sheep pen. Those sheep are your responsibility. If they get out of the pen and the Goshutes eat them, you might as well start looking for a new home. Those sheep are all the meat we have for the winter, unless I can find someone who can spare a weaner from a litter of pigs. We need those sheep and their wool to keep us in clothes, too.

"I don't believe you are ever going to get any sense of responsibility. Sylvester worked like a man all day. I wish you would pay attention and learn by his example."

Nick's ears burned. He pretended to turn his full attention to the green blob on his plate.

"What did you do today, Nicky?" Ma asked, in an apologetic tone. She patted his hand lightly. Nick did not raise his hot eyes from his plate.

"Girls' work," he muttered.

CHAPTER 2

The closing prayer dragged on and on and on. Nick sat on a narrow bench squeezed between his parents. The oppressive heat bore down on him. Nick thought about God. If that prayer reached Him, He must be down at the bottom of a barrel. Nick was positive that the deep bass tone Bishop Taylor always used when he prayed was way too heavy to float up to heaven, where everyone said God was. Nick pictured in his mind a scowling-faced God, who resembled Pa, with his dark eyes and thick black eyebrows. His imaginary God was buried under all those heavy words, struggling to get out- the way the grasshopper with the broken leg had struggled, when Nick poured his lunch bucket full of dirt on it. When the prayer finally ended, the people seemed to explode from the sweltering building. Nick was pushed along with the crowd.

"Hurry," he heard a thick-waisted woman say to her tall skinny daughter. "You give the sandwiches to Paul and Barbara and the two little ones. I'll take the baby to the wagon to change and feed him. We don't have any time to waste if we want to get through before Sacrament Meeting begins." She scurried off to her wagon to feed her wriggling sweating baby beneath a suffocating quilt.

"Did you save any of your grain?" asked a farmer, as he settled his straw hat on his head. He and his companion made a beeline to the rear of the church building. Nick usually went with them, to lean on the pole fence beside them while they talked and smoked. He liked the grown-up smell of tobacco and shaving soap that hovered about them. The smokers were not the men who ran the church, but they were friendly. Nick liked to imitate their talk, punctuated liberally with profanity. But today he needed to talk to the other boys.

He passed two little boys, rolling each other around on the ground, wrestling and swearing. Nick sort of liked most Sundays. Well, he didn't really like church, with its long-winded preachers, but he liked to see all the kids. Two years ago, when everybody had to live inside the walls at Fort Grantsville, while the Indians finished burning the farmhouses, he got to know the other boys pretty well. He could hardly wait to tell his best friend, Sam Taylor, about his adventure of last week.

"The Indians really liked me. They let me ride their horses," Nick boasted to Sam and the two Clark boys, Bub and Deke, who pressed close to hear.

"You're a dirty liar, Nick Wilson," Sam Taylor said emphatically. "I cut posts with Sylvester every single day, and he never said nothin' about no wild Injuns at your place."

"It's the truth," said Nick. "Cross my heart! They wanted to take me to Great Salt Lake City to their rendezvous. They said I was the best white boy they ever saw. They thought I would be a good Indian."

"Oh sure! And when they got you out in the desert, off goes your scalp and it's Goodbye Nick Wilson." Sam shoved Nick away from him, nearly knocking him down. "You're a no good liar."

"Injun lover! Squaw man!" Deke Clark screamed. He spat with practiced accuracy. A horrible, slimy wet blob landed right in Nick's eyes.

Nick wiped his shirtsleeve across his face. "You son of a bitch," he said. Then carefully and deliberately he aimed a kick at the spot where it would do the most damage. His loose sole caught on Deke's pant leg and spoiled Nick's aim. He only grazed Deke's knee.

"Oh! You want to fight dirty, eh?" Deke hissed between clenched teeth. He leaped at Nick knocking him flat, and piled on top of him.

"Get him, boys! Show him what we do to liars," whooped Sam gleefully. He sat heavily on Nick while his two accomplices each grabbed a leg and tugged the scratchy, baggy pants from Nick's squirming hips. Nick was bare from his waist to his shoes. The spitter, Deke, rolled the trousers into a loose wad and heaved them to the roof of the out-door privy that served the men of the church.

14

Wheezing strains of music from the pump organ inside the church called the faithful back to worship. Nick's pals abandoned him and fled to the protection of the crowd.

Nick sat, shielded by a sagebrush, until the churchyard was vacant with everyone gathered inside.

"Elijah Nicholas Wilson!" Nick's mother whispered fiercely, from the door of the church. "You come here this minute."

Nick hunkered down behind the brush, not daring to breathe. Ma only waited a second or two, just long enough so she could tell Pa that she tried to find him. Then she disappeared inside the building. When he was sure that she would not come out again, Nick rescued his pants and put them on. He sure wasn't going back into that hot box of a church and let those bastards mock him—not even to get his hat. He inched on his knees and elbows, with his belly close to the ground, until he could no longer see the church. Then he ran. He avoided the road although there was no one to see him. At home he cut a thick slice of bread from the meager hoard Ma kept in a tin box on the shelf. He drizzled the slice carefully and liberally with the sticky honey Ma was saving. He knew he shouldn't but this was Fast Sunday and he hadn't eaten since last night. Besides, he was going to catch it anyway when Pa got home.

*

After Sylvester and Pa left for Taylor's place to cut posts Monday morning, Nick sneaked back to the house with the two fish he had caught the day before. Ma knew he'd broken the Sabbath by working—that's what she called fishing—but she took the fish anyway. Nick was glad that they would have fish flavoring in the pig-weed greens tonight. The bribe was partially successful, but Ma had to say something to him about his transgressions the day before, and Pa wasn't speaking to him.

"Why did you leave church, yesterday?" Ma asked.

"Oh, those stupid boys took my pants away and threw them on top of the outhouse. I couldn't get them down 'til church started.

And I didn't want to be late, so I just came home." Nick hunched his shoulders and looked contritely at his shoes.

"Your pa was upset with you. Nick, you really should be a good example for those boys," she said.

"Aw, Ma. You don't understand," Nick said.

"You must remember, your name is Nicholas. I named you that because it means 'The People's Victory'. When you were born, you were so tiny I was afraid you would die. But you showed everyone that you were victorious. Nicky, you shouldn't fight with those boys."

Ma is such a nag, Nick thought, as he left the house. He would never say so out loud. He didn't want to hurt her feelings. He loved her most of the time. But she was always harping on that same thing. *"Your name means 'People's Victory' so be victorious."* That was so dumb. If she had named him Saint Peter, that didn't mean he would tend the pearly gates. Nick knew he wouldn't ask again to go with Pa. That didn't mean he liked to watch those confounded sheep any better. He did not want to be reminded again of Pandy's death. But he hated the loneliness. He wouldn't even mind Sylvester, who thought he was Pa when Pa wasn't there. Any company would be welcome.

Nick sat on the large granite boulder he called Overlook Rock. Old Carney and the ewes grazed placidly among the sagebrush beside it. Nick and Pandy had pretended the sheep were white men's horses. They practiced driving them stealthily through the brush. Old Carney didn't drive too well. He had a mind of his own. Pa said he acted a lot like Nick.

While Nick reminisced, he rolled a length of willow branch on the rock. He decided he might as well make a whistle. He had cut the branch carefully with the small penknife he kept in the pouch on his shoestring belt. He loved the little knife with its two tiny blades that folded neatly into the pearl handle. It had belonged to Grandpa Kiley. Nick hadn't really meant to steal it. Ma said it would be

Nick's when he learned to read. But he couldn't wait, and now Ma thought the knife was lost. Anyway, he could read most of the ABCs.

To the east, a puff of rapidly approaching dust caught Nick's attention. When it came closer, Nick saw that it was the Indian who had given him the pony ride last week. Now the man rode alone and led the small pinto mare that Nick had admired. The pile of buffalo robes was gone. One lone robe was rolled and tied to the packsaddle.

A thrill charged through Nick. He hastily returned the knife to his pouch beside Pa's awl and three fishhooks. Jumping to his feet, he yelled and waved, while the willow stick rolled from to the boulder to the ground, discarded.

The Indian tethered the horses and climbed up Overlook Rock, to Nick's side. He looked bold and wild, his chest bare and bronze. He wore fringed leather leggings, a breach clout and beautifully beaded moccasins. At his waist in a sheath hung a long knife. Nick looked at his own shoes with the sole still hanging loose. He would have liked to throw away his shoes and go barefoot in spite of the rattlesnakes, but Pa had said "No. Shoes cost money."

The man squatted on his heels beside the eager boy. "Greetings, boy who talks with the tongue of an Indian," he said in the language that was so like the Goshutes that Nick knew.

"Who are you? Are you a Goshutes?" Nick asked.

"I am called Toosnamp. I am a man with a mission. My tribe is the Shoshone. We live to the north. We feast on the bighorn sheep that climb the high mountains. We are brave beyond belief. We have many horses and the best hunting grounds. Our enemies, the Crows, live in fear of us. Our women and children are always happy."

What a strange thing to say, thought Nick. But he was glad for the company, anyway.

Toosnamp entertained Nick with stories of hunting trips along a distant river called The Wind. In that far-off land, life was constantly exciting and no one ever had to work. When the sheep shaded up in

17

the afternoon heat, Nick rode the pinto all by himself. Back and forth he rode; up and down the trail, while time raced.

"The pony will be all yours, if you will come with me," the Indian man said, as he finally lifted Nick from the horse. "Every Shoshone child has his own horse. You could be a Shoshone brave."

A strange quietness hung over them. No bleats, no bells. Suddenly Nick knew something was wrong. The sheep were gone. His scalp tightened with fear.

"I have to go," he said to the Indian. *"Oh, LORD, don't let the Goshutes get those sheep,"* he prayed as he ran and hopped toward home. His shoe sole dragged in the dirt.

"If you would like this pony to be your own, come to this place when the moon is high," his new friend called after Nick's retreating back. "I will wait by the willows."

*

"Nick, where have you been?" Ma screamed when she saw him coming. She flapped her apron wildly in a futile attempt to push the wayward ram and his flock from the garden, where they munched greedily on the unexpected bounty. "Can't you ever do anything right?"

Nick didn't answer her. He ducked his head and doggedly drove the sheep into their pen and carefully fastened the gate. He then gathered sagebrush for the fire, carried water from the creek to fill the copper boiler. He even milked the cow without being told. But in the trampled garden, topless carrots and broken cornstalks bore mute testimony to his carelessness.

"You know the rules," Pa said as he surveyed the ruin of the garden that evening. "When you won't work, you don't eat. You haven't been worth your salt lately."

Nick wished Pa would use the willow switch on him, out behind the lean-to. That would be easier than the bleak disapproval on his face.

"What the sheep ruined today would have fed us for months next winter. We don't need that kind of help. You had better go to bed now."

Nick lay awake for long hours. Despair swelled in his chest and unshed tears stung his eyes. Through the open window he saw the moon rise over the mountain.

Silently he dressed, put his Indian bow over his arm, and slipped out the window. *One less mouth to feed.* That was his atoning gift to Pa.

At the moonlit willow bunch Toosnamp waited, ready for travel. He tossed Nick easily to the small mare's back and turned away. That treacherous shoe sole snagged the pony's flank and set her dancing. The man whirled back. His long knife was instantly in his hand. Nick's heart contracted. He couldn't even run away from home without causing trouble. He shut his eyes tightly and waited to die.

CHAPTER 3

Toosnamp swished the long sharp knife and sliced off the offending sole, neatly and permanently. Nick's shoe was beyond repair. Not only had he let the sheep eat the garden, but his shoe was ruined and new shoes cost money. Now Pa would never want him back.

Nick straddled the packsaddle and clung tight. Urging his own horse and leading the pinto mare, the Indian guided them swiftly into the desert. Before dawn they stopped beside a small salty pool near the Great Salt Lake. Nick's legs pained him. He'd sat astride the horse so long his knees refused to straighten out. Deep inside him his rumbling gurgling belly reminded him that he had missed his supper. He ate greedily of the dried meat and berries from the leather pouch Toosnamp gave him. Then his head dropped forward and Nick slept where he sat.

Hours later he awoke to find himself settled on the dark curly buffalo robe.

"Time to travel," Toosnamp said.

Nick tried to pull himself to his feet. His joints throbbed and pain radiated through his inner thighs. "My legs hurt," he said, hurriedly brushing the tears from his eyes.

"This will fix you up." Toosnamp pointed to the nearby pool. He helped Nick to his feet. "Take off your pants and jump in."

Nick gingerly pulled the baggy pants from his aching legs. Great patches of skin went with them. The rough woolen pants and the packsaddle had been like sandpaper, rubbing his legs raw and bleeding. Nick held his breath and jumped, plunging to his waist in the warm salty pool.

With a savage whoop he leaped out again. He forgot the stiffness of his legs. He knew now what it meant to put salt into wounds. He howled and leaped about, beating his bare shanks trying to stamp out the burning fire in his thighs. He threw himself to the salt-encrusted ground beside the water and kicked and thrashed, screaming in agony. When the terrible searing pain finally subdued into a pulsing ache, he couldn't walk; he couldn't he couldn't even stand to put his britches on. Nick sat on his bare behind. Great sobs of pain and sorrow shook his body. He wished with all his heart that he was home.

For three days Toosnamp and Nick traveled at night. They rode beside the lake with its shimmery shore of salt. Then they struck out across a stretch of brittle yellow grass and grey spicy-smelling sagebrush. Finally, a rugged barren desert of black rubble radiated the scorching sun back to them. The foot-sore horses picked their way delicately along the rocky trail.

The buffalo sleeping robe, spread over the packsaddle on the pinto's back, allowed Nick to ride more easily. He had not put his pants on again, choosing instead to sit on them. Now they were gone—lost somewhere back along the trail. The beaten path they followed wound among rocks, across brooks and eventually led them to the brink of a high stark bluff. Spread below them on the green meadow, were miles of tepees, a city made of animal skins.

"Is this the biggest Indian camp in the word?" asked Nick. His voice was hoarse with fear. *Have I been brought here to be sacrificed to some red man's idol?* He tugged his grey shirt lower to cover his exposed legs.

The Indian beside him threw back his head and roared with laughter, as if he could read Nick's mind. "You have no reason to fear. You did not come this far to become a scalp. This is the Shoshone grand encampment. Real People do this sometimes, when it becomes important. Now we need a new tribal chief. The last chief is an ancient grandfather who wants only to make arrows for the young warriors. He is too tired to lead them into battle if it should become necessary. A council of the wise ones of the Shoshone nation will also name our hunting grounds for us. We are too many to travel together and camp together in one camp. We divide into many smaller bands to travel many different ways. Then there shall be grass enough for our horses and food and clothing for our children."

As he talked, Toosnamp guided Nick's pony slowly down the black well-trodden path, over the rocky ledge and into camp.

With so many Indians around, will I ever hear anyone speak English again? Nick wondered silently.

A cry rang through the village. "God's messenger has arrived."

Nick wasn't sure he had heard right, He looked all around. He didn't see anyone who looked like he thought an angel should. Only buckskin-clad women and children and about a hundred dogs came running from all directions. *These can't be angels,* Nick thought.

The noisy troop jogged behind Nick and Toosnamp as they threaded their way among the tepees. When they pulled their horses to a stop before a large tent, the chattering crowd pushed close around them. A young man, who towered over Toosnamp, came from the tepee.

"Welcome," he said. He was smooth faced and Nick guessed that he was about twenty-five years old.

Toosnamp dismounted and lifted Nick from the pinto. "The Gods decree a child for the ancient grandmother," he said. Then he placed Nick's hand in the hand of the young giant.

"May heaven never rain on your hunting party," the host replied.

"The mission is finished," said Toosnamp. He struck himself on his bare chest, turned abruptly and strode away, leading both horses.

Nick didn't know what else to do so he stood where he was. *Dumb,* he thought. *This is really stupid.* Maybe *he* was who they meant was an angel. Nick knew he wasn't. He had heard his mother tell his father often enough, "What do you expect? You know that Nick is no angel."

Lifting the flap of the tepee and bending low, the young man drew Nick inside. There, sitting on the floor with her feet crossed in front of her and her eyes closed, was an old woman. Her hair was grey and her wrinkled face was dropped to her chest. She looked like she was thinking hard, or maybe praying.

23

"Mother, you have a son," the young man said quietly.

The old woman lifted her head and looked straight at Nick. He felt exposed in his old shirt with the elbows out and his worn out shoes.

""This is my own mother," the Indian man told Nick. "She is now your mother too. We are brothers from this day."

"Thank you, Washakie. You are a kind son," the woman said. "This boy needs repairing. His legs are like young willows when the porcupines have eaten. Do what you must to mend them."

The man called Washakie stooped low and left the darkened dwelling.

"Don't be afraid, little brother," the old woman said, putting her hand gently on Nick's trembling shoulder. "We will treat you well. You will grow up to be a great warrior like your brother, Washakie, that man of peace. I must now see the damage to the legs." She pulled at Nick's shirt, to lift it and see the injured shanks. Nick quickly grabbed it and yanked it back down. No female had seen him naked since he was seven.

R r r i i p p p... The whole front of Nick's shirt tore across from seam to seam, leaving it to hang in tatters past his knees. His rawhide shoestring belt and precious pouch still hung at his bare waist.

"Do it your way, if you must," the old woman said. She let go of Nick's shirt and handed him a whiskey bottle with a broken top. It was half full of a greenish, greasy salve. From the smell of it, there was no doubt it had something to do with skunks.

"You must rub this on your legs where they hurt."

"No thanks," Nick said. The bath in the salty pool had convinced him that he had had quite enough Indian medicine to last a lifetime.

"Oh yes," the old woman replied.

Without realizing how it happened, Nick found himself lying on his back. The old woman planted her ample bottom astride his chest. She vigorously rubbed the odorous mess into the scabbing thighs.

24

Nick was shattered. His shirt and shoes were ruined. His pants were gone. He had no privacy. He had no family. Homesickness swept over him. When the woman removed her bulk from his body, he flopped over on to his face and howled. Great choking sobs shook him. His chest and throat ached as if they would burst.

The woman gently dragged him by the ankles to a pile skins. He did not resist when she rolled him onto it. The fight was gone out of Nick. Tenderly, the woman sank beside him and cradled him to her. Wailing sorrowfully into his neck, she joined her sobs with his. Together they cried themselves to sleep.

*

When Nick opened his eyes, he was alone in the tepee. A delicious smell drifted through the open flap, tantalizing his nostrils. The air had a feeling of lateness. Nick rolled off his bed of skins and poked his head through the greasy flap. A fire burned merrily under a chunk of sizzling, dripping meat. The old woman crouched before the browning meat, poking the fire.

"Woman, can I have something to eat?" Nick asked, when she looked in his direction.

"The meat will soon be ready," she said. Rising, she came noiselessly into the tepee.

"Remove the rags from yourself." She pointed to the ripped grey homespun shirt Nick still wore.

"No thanks," Nick said. "I am not going to run around naked as a bare-assed papoose."

"Dress in these," the woman said, ignoring Nick's hostile remark. "I am your mother and I desire you to be clothed like a proper child. When you have again used the salve on your legs and dressed, you may eat." Turning she left Nick alone.

Nick examined the deerskin items she had laid near him. The shirt was almost pure white, as soft as his mother's best sprigged calico dress. Long leather fringes hung from the shoulders to where the shirt sleeves ended at the elbows. Across the breast, beads of blue and orange were sewn into the shapes of hearts and diamonds. Beside the shirt sat a pair of golden buckskin moccasins. They were the most beautiful clothes Nick had ever owned. Kicking off his soleless shoes and discarding his ragged shirt, Nick hastily rubbed the stinking salve into his sores and donned his new finery. The shirt reached below his knees and the high moccasins ended just beneath the shirt. They were surprisingly comfortable. Nick knotted his shoestring belt about his waist and emerged from the tepee dressed in the clothes of a Shoshone woman. He didn't know and he didn't care. He was covered.

"The council is choosing the new tribal chief," Nick's new mother told him once he had eaten until he could hot hold another bite. "The young braves watch and learn the Shoshone ways. If it would please you, I will take you there."

"You bet." Nick replied. The woman looked puzzled. "I want to," he explained. He felt ready for anything now.

In an immense clearing, larger than the walled part of Grantsville, sat the men of the tribe. The respected elders sat in the front. Around them clustered the warriors, and then the boys of Nick's age. A few women also sat and watched.

"We will sit among the council, so that you can see and hear everything." The old woman crowded herself and Nick into a small gap between two old men at the front of the throng. Good naturedly, the men squeezed together to let them in.

The council of wise men passed a tobacco pipe with a long narrow stem around the circle, skipping the old woman and Nick. Each took a puff of the aromatic pipe, sucking long at the stem, drawing the smoke into their lungs. With half-closed eyes, wearing expressions of profound knowledge and contentment, these revered tribesmen blew smoke back through flaring nostrils—only one puff each.

On their heads, they wore headdresses that appeared to be badges of their honor. Some wore bonnets of feathers, hoods of animal

26

skins. One old man had a black cooking pot turned upside down upon his head.

Stupid, thought Nick. White men took their hats off when they held a meeting, and they never, never, never smoked in a public place.

"The War Chief and the Medicine-man have already been chosen," the old woman whispered loudly to Nick. "The council is resting while they decide who will lead them. They have heard about all who are brave enough to be the Tribal Chief. They have decided against all but two. Over there, beneath the tree are the two remaining candidates."

"Isn't that your son?" asked Nick, indicating a young man who squatted on his heels, beneath the tree.

"Yes, that is your brother, Washakie. He will be a great chief."

"Who is that with him—the short fat man with all the feathers hanging down his back?" Nick pointed to a man who was pacing back and forth near Washakie.

"That is Doso Ono, Buffalo Robes his name means to the Shoshones. When he was young like Washakie, he went among the white men who lived at Fort Hall on the Paiupa River. He learned to like the white men food. He ate much pigs and sheep. When they saw how much he liked their meat the white men called him for it. They called him Pork-and-Tallow. The Indian changed it to Pocatello.

"That is when some evil white men stole away his wife and his baby son. They used his wife badly. Then they killed her and her baby. Now Doso Ono wants to be known as Pocatello, the name the white men gave him. There are many Shoshone warriors named Doso Ono, but there is only one Pocatello. He wants the white men to know that because they chose to be his enemy, he will kill them all, or drive them from the Shoshone land.

"Pocatello wants the Real People to make war against all white men. That is what they will do if Pocatello is chosen Tribal Chief."

27

Pocatello had watched with angry eyes, as the old woman had seated herself and Nick among the elders. Now he strode to where they sat. With more venomous hatred than Nick had ever known, Pocatello pointed an accusing finger at Nick and said two words.

"White Man!"

CHAPTER 4

The men of the council paid no attention to Pocatello's theatrics. Someone calmly handed a basket to a young brave. The boy carried the basket from man to man, stopping before every member of the council.

Nick hunkered down beside the old woman, trying to make himself invisible. The woman, seeming not to notice Nick's discomfort, continued to explain the process to him in a loud whisper.

"Each man of the council has been given two pebbles, a white one and a black one. If he puts a white pebble in the basket, he prefers Washakie. The black pebble is for Pocatello."

Nick watched urgently, as the oldest man of the council poured the pebbles from the basket to a red blanket that was spread in front of him. Slowly he sorted the pebbles into two piles. To Nick's immense relief, the pile of white pebbles was twice the size of the black pile. Washakie, that Man of Peace, was the new tribal chief. For a few seconds no one moved. Then Pocatello bounded into the council circle.

"Shoshone warriors are old grandmothers!" he shouted. "You let the white men take your hunting grounds and disgrace your women. I say kill the white man! But Washakie is what you deserve. May all your sons be girls." He stomped away from the council.

Here and there, throughout the gathering, men rose to their feet and followed Pocatello. Nick had seen men fight all his life. They usually went behind the blacksmith shop and hit each other in the face and belly. He even heard that sometimes, if they had been drinking strong spirits, they even shot each other. But he had never seen a man break up a meeting like Pocatello had. The men he knew always pretended that they liked what happened in a meeting even when they didn't.

"Is Pocatello going to leave the Shoshone tribe?" asked Nick, as he and the old woman returned to their tepee.

"No," the old woman said. "It might be better for the Real People if he did. Pocatello and his warriors will continue to make war against the white man, and the Real People will be blamed. But Washakie is still the tribal chief. Pocatello's band will follow the directions of the council in things that matter."

Nick was shocked. "Don't the white people matter?"

"The white men do not make it rain or snow. They do not choose our hunting grounds or instruct our children. No, little brother, the white man does not matter."

"Who are these Real People you are always talking about?" Nick asked angrily. "Isn't everybody a real person?"

"Real People know and keep the ways of the Great Spirit who dwells in the sky. The red men call our Shoshones, which means 'Eater of Sheep', because we climb to the highest peaks, where the wild sheep roam. Many lifetimes ago, the Great Spirit gave his ways to the Chief of the Shoshones when he was high on a mountain. We have since tried to follow his rules. Shoshones do not always act like Real People," the old woman concluded sorrowfully.

*

The time of the grand encampment was boisterously exciting. Every man appeared to think that he was the strongest or fastest or the best shot. Whenever two or more men got together, contests were held to prove these things. Nick noticed that a man with a red-dyed wool blanket could always find someone to race with him. They gambled for buffalo robes, horses, or bows and arrows. The metal arrowheads traded to them by the white men were valuable betting items. Many a man bet a good horse for a handful of arrowheads made from a tin bucket.

Women chatted and laughed, while they scraped away at deer hides with scrapers made from stones. Babies blinked their dark little eyes and swung form the branches of trees, where they were suspended in their little cradleboards. Kids raced around mimicking the actions of their parents. The dogs were everywhere, barking loudly. It was the noisiest place Nick could remember, even worse than Mormon Conference.

At sunset, most of the tribe gathered around the council fire. Nick looked warily around for Pocatello. He did not see him anyplace. He could not see another white person either. He was all alone surrounded by all these Indians.

"How many people are here?" he asked the Indian woman who was now his mother.

"More that last council," she replied. "As many as the antelope feeding near the Twin Buttes."

That didn't tell Nick anything. He had never seen the Twin Buttes. He didn't even know where they were. He did know that there were a lot of people here, though. Maybe ten thousand. He didn't know how many ten thousand were, but he knew it was more than he could count.

The men seated near the fire seemed in no hurry to start the meeting. Nick was used to promptness. In the white world, someone was always in charge. Here, the men just sat and visited or got up and wandered around.

Finally a warrior, splendid in his Indian finery, wearing a feathered headdress and several strands of turquoise and shell beads about his neck, stood. He chanted in a sing-song voice a story about a buffalo hunt ' Across the throng of people, a man stood to repeat every word as it was spoken. Scattered among the crowds were other men doing the same. There was no one who couldn't hear the story being told to that enormous gathering.

Another warrior told of horses stolen from the Crows. Thus it went. Stories similar to the ones told Nick on Overlook Rock were repeated to the entire tribe. Nick decided they were reciting all the gossip since the last big powwow. The Shoshone language was so similar to the Goshutes that Nick knew, that he scarcely missed a word.

31

Then Nick recognized Toosnamp's deep booming voice.

"There was an ancient grandmother," Toosnamp sang. His words echoed again and again across the gathering. "Her husband, the chief, had gone to the Happy Hunting Grounds in the sky," he continued. "She had two sons. The older was a brave warrior; the younger was still a child. The grandmother's youngest son went into the mountain to hunt. The snows roared down the mountain. He was buried beneath the avalanche. The woman mourned. The Great Spirit told her, 'The little brother of the chief will return. He will be as white as the snows that buried him.'

"Now the ancient grandmother is happy. The Great Spirit spoke wisdom. Her older son is Washakie, that Man of Peace. He is the new chief; and the brother of the chief has returned. He is as white as snow."

When Toosnamp took his seat, it seemed to Nick that all the people in the camp rose to their feet and stared at him. He squirmed beneath their eyes. *They had better not expect me to sing because I'm not going to.*

He wasn't going to lie about coming back from the dead. He was, and always had been, Nick Wilson, brother of that snitch, Sylvester.

His mind was eased when another warrior stood and the recitations continued. Only the warriors were permitted to sing.

Later, everyone—women and children included—danced. They stomped and whirled in a circle around some tall willow stakes. They whooped and chanted at the top of their lungs to the rhythm of drums.

"Oh boy," Nick enthused. "That looks great. I think I might help them with their yelling and jumping. I can do that."

"I am going to bed and so are you," said the old woman. She pointed to the tall stakes driven into the ground, where the tribe was warming up to dance all night. The tassels hanging from the stakes were not ordinary tassels. As Nick looked closely, he saw that they were made of human hair.

"You can see the scalps. Do you want yours to hang there? Some of these warriors would be glad to add your white curly wool to their collection."

"Oh, well...I'm tired anyway." Nick shuddered and his stomach churned. He swallowed hard so be would not throw up in front of everyone.

*

It was early when young voices woke him. He had slept in his clothes. His real mother would never have allowed that, but the old Indian woman hadn't undressed either. Outside some children clustered about a couple of boys. A boy who looked about eight stood with his bare feet spread wide apart. As Nick came closer, he heard a scream— not really a scream, more like a squeak.

"Oowee. Mopi, you missed."

A boy guffawed. "Oh, that is wrong. You moved. If you had not moved it would have been all right. You were cut because you moved."

"No I didn't move. You have bad aim," the little boy insisted.

"What are you doing?" Nick asked as he joined them. The small boy sank to the ground and looked at his bleeding toe.

"This is a game of skill," replied the boy who had been called Mopi. He held in his hand a hunting knife with a long blade. "Only braves with a true eye and a steady hand are allowed to play this game."

I'd like to look like him, thought Nick. He looked so...Indian. His hair was held off his forehead by a heavily beaded leather thong. Thick black braids hung over each shoulder. The hair that escaped the braids swung like a horse's tail down his back. He was bare except for a breach clout, a long piece of soft buckskin worn between the legs like a diaper and fastened to a belt. A flap hung down in front and back. His moccasins were nearly black, with a porcupine quill pattern in red and white beads sewn across the toes.

33

His bare body shone like dark mahogany.

Nick ran his fingers through his own short kinky blond hair. He looked at his own arms, which had always been shielded from sunburn. They were as white as a fish's belly. Envy swelled in him. Nick knew he could never look like that.

"What makes that such a great game?" Nick asked. Envy sounded a lot like sarcasm. "I bet I could play it. I am good at games. I can do anything you can."

"If you want to know this game, take off your moccasins and I will show you how we do it." Mopi gestured at Nick's feet.

"Yes. Take off your moccasins and Mopi will show you," said the little boy who sat on the ground. He curled himself into a ball and licked the blood off his toe.

"No you won't, Mopi. You will get into trouble," a girl said. She stepped between Nick and Mopi. It was the girl who had giggled behind her hands at the willow bunch back home. She didn't giggle now. A cross little line between her eyebrows made it plain that she didn't feel at all like laughing.

"He wants you to spread your feet wide apart so you can't jump away, while he tosses a knife at them," the girl told Nick. "The game is to get close to your toes without hitting them. But Mopi always misses. He cuts everyone he plays with. If he cut you, your mother would kill him."

"Raida, you go away," Mopi said. He pushed the girl. "Boys do not want you to be where they are."

"You are mean, Mopi. You want me to go so you can be cruel. I will tell Mother that you want to be a dog stealer. You do not want to belong to the Real People." Raida turned and ran to a tepee that stood close by, across a small stream.

Nick watched Raida go, then turned back to the boys. "I have played your silly game a hundred times. We call it 'Stretch'," he boasted. "Let me borrow your knife, Mopi, and I will put it through your moccasin and never touch your toe." Nick hoped these boys would not know that he was bluffing. But better Mopi's toe than his. He had seen this game played at home. Some of the fellows were so good at 'Stretch' that they could plant a knife between your toes and never even scratch you. The only time he had played it, Sylvester threw the knife at Nick's toe. Nick knew his would be gone if he hadn't jumped. Nick was betting that Mopi would not let him get his hands on that knife anyway.

"What are you called?" asked Mopi, changing the subject.

"My name is Nick. It means People's Victory. The old woman calls me Brother. Say, why are you called Mopi? Doesn't Mopi mean 'Came Last'? I think you would be called 'Came First!'"

Mopi turned his back to Nick and refused to answer.

"Mopi and Raida were born together," a boy who stood nearby told Nick. "They are twins. The medicine man said Raida should be put to death because she would steal Mopi's medicine, but her mother said NO. Raida is the oldest and she does everything like a boy. She races horses, she throws the lariat, she shoots arrows. She steals Mopi's medicine, and she makes Mopi ashamed. But she won't tell on him."

Mopi turned back to Nick, his face dark with anger. "You talk a lot, Boni. This child should not hear about Shoshone ways. He faced his friend. "This is not the brother of the chief. He is a white boy who talks like an Indian. This is the white boy I saw on the way to the rendezvous. Washakie traded three of his horses to my father for a pinto mare. Toosnamp gave the pinto to this boy so he would come with him. The old woman wanted a white boy and this boy is it. This boy should be called Yagaiki, the Crier. He is a baby. He can not even ride a horse."

Mopi grabbed Nick's long shirt and lifted it high for everyone to see his scabbing legs. Furiously, Nick kicked with all his strength. He aimed high and his aim was good. He caught Mopi right in his round dark belly. Mopi tumbled backward; his head bounced on the hard ground. Nick had kicked the breath out of him. Mopi lay

35

sprawled on his back for a long minute. Then he jumped up, blood trickling from his nose. Clutching his stomach, he dashed to his tepee bawling loudly.

Women's heads popped out of surrounding dwellings. Each woman called shrilly at her own child. The children wasted no time. They rapidly fled to the safety of their tepees. From the tepee Mopi and Raida had entered came a woman clutching a long butcher knife. Mopi's mother swished the air wickedly and headed straight for Nick.

"You vile little son of a white man! If you want blood you will get blood!" she screamed. "I will cut out your heart before you are an hour older!"

Nick backed against the tepee. He stood with doubled fists, waiting, ready for the woman's charge. If he was going to die, he was going out fighting.

The old woman who was his new mother poked her head from the flap of her lodge. Catching the back of his shirt, the old woman hauled Nick inside.

"Foolish boy," she scolded him loudly. "Do you want to get yourself killed again?

CHAPTER 5

"I need to ask you something," Nick said the day after his fight with Mopi.

"You are to say anything you want," the old woman told him.

"What am I supposed to call you? Toosnamp called you Ancient Grandmother but that seems so...old."

"Ancient Grandmother is a name of respect for older women. Washakie calls me Mother. You are Washakie's brother now. If you want to, you can call me Mother, too." The old woman smiled at him.

"No. That won't do. My mother lives in Grantsville, in the Utah territory. Her name is Janet Kiley Wilson. I love her a lot. You aren't my mother!" Nick felt his face burning. His mother was kind. She hadn't objected when he played with Pandy all the time. She was glad when Pa brought Pandy's family to live nearby and help with the chores on the farm. All that the Goshutes family wanted was food and a place to pitch their tepee for protection against the raiders. Some people, both Indian and white hated it when Indians and white people were friends. But his mother was glad to give Pandy's family a place to live in exchange for their labor.

But Ma wouldn't want her son to actually *be* an Indian. She would not want anyone to think *she* wore smelly blankets and squatted on the ground to cook her meals. She wouldn't want anyone to think that *she* was a heathen. Nick felt like a traitor to even think of calling this wrinkled old dark-skinned woman *Mother*.

"No," he said again. "That won't do. If you don't mind, I think I will call you 'M'lady'. That's what my Ma says you are supposed to call the woman who is the mother or wife of the president. It is a name of respect, too. Washakie is sort of the president of the Shoshones so I will call you M'lady."

"When I was a young wife, I had a daughter. She was a little girl of beauty. I was happy to be her mother. When she was six summers old, she fell from her horse and died. After awhile Washakie, that

Man of Peace, was born to me. He was a serious child, always obeying his father, the chief. He was trained to be a chief from the time he was small. He was a good boy, always fair to everyone. When he grew older I had another son, a laughing, playful child. This was the child of my old age. This was the child of my heart.

"After his father was killed in the Great War with the Crows, the child became restless. This was in the winter just past. He went into the mountains to hunt the sheep and the Great Spirit. When he did not return, I went in search of him. He was under the snow, but his legs were not covered. The wolves had gnawed at the flesh of his legs. They left the bones showing. When HE returned you to me, the Great Spirit had covered the places where the wolves had chewed the flesh away… But he left large sores on your legs. It was a sign to me so that I might know that you are my true child.

"I am truly your mother. However, if you do not want to call me Mother, M'lady will do very well. It is a nice name. If in white man's tongue it means Mother of the Chief, I will be M'lady to you."

*

No one actually declared the encampment over. Several days later, people merely loaded their belongings on their horses and rode away. Over a week's time, they drifted out of the meadows, in bands of two or three hundred—enough for protection, but not too many to feed.

"Get up, Brother. Today we are going to travel," M'lady said one morning. Nick watched while the elk-skin covering of the tepee dropped to the ground with a dull thud. The old woman, with efficiency and skill, folded and rolled the covering that lay around the pole skeleton of her home. Next, she attacked the lacings that held the poles together.

"Where are we going?" asked Nick.

"We must go to the Big Hole Basin where we will remain through the winter. It is many days' travel. We must before hurry for we still have much food to collect and prepare before the snows.

"Can't I help?" asked Nick. At home, everyone pitched into the job when there was work at hand.

"Women care for the lodge and the family. Men provide the food and fight the battles." M'lady outlined the Indian code. "I have prepared the lodge for the move since I came as a girl to live in the house of Washakie's father. I must do it so it will be done right. You stay back, then the poles will not hit you as they fall."

"I want to help." Nick was restless. The whole camp was bustling all around him. They were the last bunch to leave, but he was only in the way.

"Take your food pouch and eat and rest up for the long journey," the woman told him. She pushed him gently out of her way.

I might as well not be here, Nick thought. She treats me like I was a baby.

At M'lady's insistence, Nick had ridden his pinto every day since his arrival. He needed to toughen the skin on his legs, she said. She had been right. His legs had grown firm and supple. Now he had a long trip ahead of him. He might as well get his horse. M'lady didn't let him go to the horse pasture unless accompanied by her, Toosnamp or Washakie. But he went there as often as he could get someone to go with him. His horse now came to him when he called her. He sure did love that horse. He wished he could spend more time with her.

Nick felt like a prisoner in the large tepee. When he asked to so play with the kids, the old woman told him stories of children who had been stolen away and taken where they would never See their mothers again.

"You must never go out alone," she said. "You do not know what a child stealer looks like. I am your mother and I would not be happy if you were stolen away."

But now everyone except members of their very own band were gone. Nick wasn't afraid of *them*. Besides, they were all busy today.

39

Nick took the rawhide hackamore he used to catch his pony and strolled off to the horse pasture. At least his pinto would be glad to see him.

In the pasture, no pony whinnied to welcome him. The horse pasture was nearly empty, and his pinto mare wasn't there. Three boys were over at the far end. They worked their way among the scattered horses, to separate their own from the diminishing herd. As they came closer, Nick saw that one of the boys was Mopi, the boy he had kicked in the belly.

"Have you seen my horse?" Nick asked, trying to be friendly. If they were going to be in the same camp, they may as well get along.

"It must have run away in the night," Mopi said. He winked and grinned at the two boys with him.

"Where would a horse go?" Nicked wondered out loud.

"Who can guess?" one of the other boys said. He winked back at Mopi.

"It won't be far," the third boy said. "Horses do not travel fast through the lavas. They could step in a hole and break their legs."

Raida stood a little way from the boys, holding three horses by their halters. She glared at her brother and shook her head.

"I am going after my horse," Nick decided.

"You had better ask your mother," Mopi taunted. "What does little Yagaiki who gets sore legs from riding know about horses?"

"Nick's face flooded with color. In that instant he felt very small. He wished he was back home in Grantsville. He deserved to be called Crier. He had bawled more since he left home than he had since he was a baby. But nobody was going to call him names without a fight.

"You shut up! You just shut up!" shouted Nick. "YOU aren't so great. Your place is right after the girls."

Mopi leaped to the back of the horse he was holding by the neck. Although he had no reins, Mopi, guiding the horse by its mane, galloped full speed at Nick.

40

Nick remembered that the blacksmith at Grantsville had once told him that when a horse has his eyes open he will not run into anything. It is when they buck that they close their eyes and run into things. That big roan charging down on Nick had its eyes open. Nick waited, and when it got almost upon him, Nick stepped back and the horse swerved away from him.

"Run, Yagaiki!" roared Mopi.

Nick couldn't help himself. He whirled and ran. Blindly he left behind the camping ground, now sparsely covered by tepees, and raced up the well-worn track. Hatred for Mopi burned inside him, driving him into the lava beds.

When a growing stitch in his side forced him to slow his headlong dash, he remembered the missing pony. But the black rocky waste was empty. Nick trudged forlornly but determinedly up the trail. Somewhere in this desolation, his poor pony was lost. She heeded him. And he needed her. Every Shoshone in the whole nation had at least one horse. But now he didn't have any. Now he guessed he would have to go back to Grantsvilled and tend sheep. Maybe that would be all right. He wasn't having much fun being an Indian anyway. He was always fighting with Mopi, and the old woman didn't let him out of her sight. He didn't get to go hunting deer or buffalo or even jackrabbits. He might as well go home. His mother would be glad to see him. Then he remembered. He couldn't go back. He didn't have any shoes and Ma hated moccasins. He didn't have anything to eat either. The sheep had eaten it all. Besides Pa always said, "If you ever run away, don't bother to come back."

Nick blinked back tears and kept on walking.

Clip-clop. Clip-clop.

Behind him Nick heard a horse picking its way carefully through the rocks. He turned hopefully but it wasn't his pinto. A warrior riding a large bay horse came from the direction of the Indian villiage. He rode his horse up to Nick and stopped.

"What is the brother of the Chief doing so far from home?"

asked the warrior.

"My horse has wandered away and I am looking for it," Nick told him. Nick was glad that the man was a Shoshone from the same camp as he was.

"What kind of a horse is it?" the man asked.

"It's a brown and white pinto, but she is wearing hobbles on her front feet. She couldn't be very far away."

"Maybe the hobbles broke or maybe the Crows cut them off. They sometimes do that when no one is watching. Climb up behind me. I will take you over the next hill. You can see if your horse is there."

Nick caught the offered hand and allowed himself to be pulled onto the horse behind the warrior. He really needed to catch his pony. They rode over the first hill. They crossed the second and third hill. They were getting farther and farther from camp. The warrior looked over his shoulder, checking behind. Then he whipped his horse into a gallop. Didn't he know his horse could break its legs in the lavas?

"You had better slow down," Nick said.

The man whipped his horse harder, trying to get more speed.

"Hey! Where are you taking me?" Nick shouted.

"I see a band of horses over the next hill," the Indian answered.

Nick looked and saw nothing but barren waste. "Where are you taking me?" Nick demanded again.

The warrior laid his quirt to the horse, over and under, and said nothing.

"Hey, let me off!" Nick roared. He was getting scared.

When the horse slowed slightly, and scrambled for footing in the rough twisting trail, Nick saw his chance. He propelled himself backward over the rump, somersaulting to the ground. He landed on his shoulders and jumped hastily to his feet. He hesitated only an instant to see what his captor would do about that. The Indian pulled on his horse. He was obviously not ready to have his prisoner escape that easily.

Nick fled down the trail toward home while the old woman's stories of child stealers flooded back to his mind. His senses warned him that he could not outrun the galloping horse. His only hope was to leave the established path and run into the fractured tumbled wasteland. Maybe the warrior would be afraid to follow him, or maybe the horse would break its legs if he did follow.

Behind him, Nick heard hooves pounding toward him on the hard ground and he knew he had to act fast. With a burst of speed Nick leaped from the path and ran with total abandon, into the lava flow. He darted from rock pile to buckbrush seeking a safe place to hide. The warrior left his horse on the trail and with whip in hand tracked Nick through the rough. He was closing in. Nick knew he had no hope of escape. Suddenly the ground dropped from under him and Nick was plunged from the face of the earth.

CHAPTER 6

Nick landed with a thump. Dust puffed up around him in a blinding cloud. When it settled back, he was shrouded in the fine dry powder. Coughing, he sat up, his eyes gradually growing accustomed to the dim light. He sat in an underground room that was at least twice as long as he was tall. Porous rock walls sloped up to the low ceiling, no higher than Nick's head. He sat in a lava-rock bubble. The only opening was the crack in the lava just above his head, through which he had fallen. The floor beneath him was covered in the dust and debris that had sifted down in the eons since the rock dome had been formed by molten lava.

A rustling sound caught Nick's attention. It was so faint that he doubted his own ears. A pebble rattled against a rock. His pursuer was nearby, maybe right overhead. Nick inched silently from beneath the hole to the furthest place in the cave. There he scrunched down against the wall, not even breathing.

"Don't be afraid, little rabbit," crooned the Indian in a sing-song voice. "You can trust your friend. I only want to help you."

Nick waited, crouched in the darkness. He was pretty sure that that Indian wasn't his friend, and he was positive he didn't trust him.

"Come out, you skinny rabbit." The warrior sounded cross now. "Come out! This hungry coyote wants to eat you."

That's what I thought. Well if that coyote wants to eat this rabbit, he will have to dig for me, thought Nick.

Overhead, the grunting and mumbling drew closer. A Shadow darkened the hole. A bare arm reached inside, a hand at the end, grabbing the air here and there.

"I have you now." The warrior chuckled maliciously. "There is no way for you to escape."

The arm stretched in Nick's direction, and Nick tried to press himself through the rough black wall. An eerie, cackling laugh echoed through the cavern, followed by a flapping rustle.

"Yee-oww!" the Indian shrieked, and yanked his arm from the

hole. "I know who you are, you devil bird," said the Indian above Nick's hiding place. "You are the Brother of the Chief. Do not spirit me away. I did not want to hurt you. I do not want a firestick. I am a friend to all spirits and ghosts. I do not want a herd of horses."

While this pleading voice talked on, it moved further and further from Nick's hole in the lavas. In a few seconds, Nick heard a horse's hooves clattering in the rocks as it galloped away. Then silence.

If this was a trick to make him show himself, Nick wasn't going to fall for it. He sat with his back to the wall, his eyes glued to the crack in the top of his hiding place. There he silently waited.

He heard nothing for some time, then a whistling, scratching noise whispered faintly through the small room. Nick was at once alert to the murmuring and muffled rustling near the opening. *If that Indian is waiting for me there, he will have a long wait.* Nick's Pa said he was a stubborn boy. Right now, Nick was glad he was. He was sure going to be stubborn now.

After a few moments, when no more sounds were heard, Nick relaxed. He could hear his stomach growling. He remembered the food pouch that he had left for M'lady to fill with fresh food for their journey. That seemed like hours ago.

I will starve down here, in this hole, and no one will ever find me, Nick thought. I guess if that coyote Indian wants to eat me, he might just as well try it. I'll kick his head off. But I'm getting out of this hole.

Nick crept cautiously to the crack in the dome and stood carefully. He didn't hear anything. Nothing grabbed him. He reached out of the hole and grasped the sagebrush that grew there. Using the bush for leverage, he hoisted himself from his prison. With his belly on the edge of his escape hole, Nick looked straight into the face of...

A white ground owl. The bird, startled, gave the eerie cackling laugh Nick had heard earlier when the Indian was reaching into the hole after Nick. The frightened bird flapped to a pile of rubble close to the hole. Beneath the sagebrush was a nest with three half-feathered young owls. Cheeping like baby chicks, they hopped a sideways hop to get away from Nick.

Nick laughed out loud. "I'm not going to hurt you, nor your precious babies. I want to thank you for saving my life. That old coyote would have had me for sure if you hadn't scared him. He probably thought I'd turned into an owl and flown away. You can come back to your babies now. I'm not a ghost and neither are you. I'm going to go get something to eat."

Nick trotted back down the path toward the meadow. Someone with a blanket over the head came trudging up the trail. Nick slowed warily, but continued toward whoever it was.

"Ooo-wee, ooo-wee. I have lost my little boy. Pocatello stole him. If I don't find him, I shall die." It was M'lady. She plodded slowly up the trail, dragging the hackamore Nick had dropped at the horse pasture. When she looked up and saw Nick, she fairly flew to him.

For such an old woman, she sure can move, thought Nick.

"Oh, my cruel boy," she cried. Big tears trickled down her wrinkled face. "Do you want to cause your old mother's death? If you go away I shall surely die of grief."

Nick allowed her to hug him to her and smash his face into her smelly armpit. She had hugged him more in the week he had been with her, than he had been hugged in his life. He guessed maybe if she loved him that much, she really might die if he left.

"Why did you go away?" M'lady asked him.

"I couldn't find my horse. My pinto is lost," Nick said. "I needed to find her."

"You look in all the wrong places," M'lady said. "The pinto is waiting for you beside the packhorses. Washakie brought it from the pasture with the rest of the horses." The old woman put her arm around Nick and pulled him close t0 her again. But she kept right on scolding him.

When they reached the horses, standing packed and ready to

47

travel, she turned to her grown son. "Washakie, this cruel boy did not tell me when he went away with that dog stealer, Pocatello, to be killed. If that twin girl, Raida, had not seen it, he would be gone forever."

"No, I wouldn't," said Nick. "That warrior was not Pocatello. Besides, I got away from him by myself. I didn't even see Pocatello. That warrior said he was going to help me find my horse. If he'd wanted to scalp me, I would already be dead."

Nick looked questioningly at Washakie. "He told me he didn't want a firestick or a herd of horses. What did he want from me?"

Washakie laughed. He put his arm affectionately around Nick's shoulder. "You are growing in value, little brother. We traded three horses for your pinto so you would come with us. Now, that warrior thought he could trade you for a whole herd of horses or a gun." Then Washakie looked serious. "You must be very careful, Brother. That warrior *was* one of Pocatello's band. Pocatello and his warriors are angry with me because I do not think it would be wise to fight with the white men. If Pocatello and his warriors could make trouble between the red, and the white men by selling you to the Sioux for a firestick, they would do so. The Sioux make a practice of stealing white children and selling them back to the white men's army for guns or horses. Then they blame the Shoshones for stealing the children. The army will come against the Shoshones to make war. In that way, Pocatello will show that he is right to hate the white men.

"Do not go away with anyone again. Mother wants to keep you for a while." Washakie stroked his chin thoughtfully. "Mother," he said. "This boy must be made busy. You should let him help you around the camp until he learns the Shoshone ways. If he lives long enough, he may learn to be one of the Real People."

*

When Washakie's band of Indians left the meadow to meander toward the winter range, Nick found himself surrounded by packhorses, doing the work of a girl. At least he was riding a horse,

48

guiding the pack string up the trail; not dragging behind one, on a travois made of lodge poles, like sick people or the babies.

The men and boys rode in a large loose circle, herding the unbroken horses, about a mile ahead of the women with the pack animals. The camp traveled like a large disjointed swarm of ants, scattered over three or four miles. Every person followed the one in front of him. Each one carried his appointed burden as the column pushed steadily to the north.

Nick thought of Washakie out in front of the crush, away from the flies and the dust. Nick would have liked to be there with the other boys, galloping up and down along the herd of horses. If he wasn't afraid he would be stolen again, maybe he could talk M'lady into letting him ride there. But he guessed this was all right. Nick liked horses.

There didn't seem to be much planning in the movement of the Indians. They traveled for a few days, then stopped and pitched their tents and rested a day or two. Each day the scouts brought freshly killed venison for the whole camp. The women cut the uneaten portion of the meat into long narrow strips and hung it in the smoke of a smoldering fire until it looked and tasted like a piece of sagebrush.

"I must leave for a while," Washakie said one evening. "A messenger came today from Hamori's camp, to the east of us. The Crows have stolen many of his people's horses. He desires that I come to meet with him to discuss what should be done. This camp will remain here, beside the river until I return. The elk are plentiful in the lodge-pole forest to the west. Toosnamp will bring you elk enough to keep you working. Brother, you are to help Mother. Do whatever she requests."

Nick was glad for the stop. He had wandered to the river after the tepee was up. The fish jumping in the eddy near shore glinted silvery in the rays of the setting sun. He had not used his fishhooks since he left Grantsville. The old familiar urge to go fishing filled his

49

thoughts.

At daylight he was up. Quickly he gathered enough wood to keep the fire in M'lady's smoke tent smoldering. He pulled a few hairs from his pinto's tail. He cut a willow with his little penknife, exactly right for a fishing pole. When he returned to their tepee, M'lady was stretching and yawning, enjoying the luxury of a day without travel.

"I want to go to the river to fish for a while. I will bring some fish for you to smoke, too. You can cook me a fish for my dinner."

"You come when I call," said M'lady. "Go now and catch a bunch of fish."

Nick baited his hook with a crunchy fat grasshopper. He tossed it into the eddy. Fish were waiting hungrily for it. As soon as it touched the water, a fish grabbed the grasshopper. With a yank, Nick had the fish flopping on the bank beside him. Several dark-eyed children had gathered to watch. Nick rapidly pulled fish after fish from the river, to add to the growing pile on the bank.

"Let me do that," said the little boy who had his toe cut playing Stretch.

"What are you called?" asked Nick.

"He is Gowani, Running Chipmunk," said a girl who was a little taller than Nick. "I am Patooli, which means Shell Flower. Can we do that with the fish, too?"

"All right," said Nick. He handed Patooli the pole he was holding and showed her how to tell when a fish took the hook. "We need more bait, Gowani. You go catch some grasshoppers. I have more hooks. We will get a couple more poles ready."

Nick motioned to two boys his own age who had joined the group. In a few minutes Nick, Boni, and Yagamont had rigged two more poles for his extra hooks. Three kids fished at a time, Nick was surprised at how willingly they shared.

"What is this?" asked Mopi, as he raced up to where Boni was pulling a silvery pink fish from the water. Mopi bumped Boni hard in the middle of his back. Into the water went Boni, pole, fish, and all.

"Ooo-wee, you pushed me!" Boni said, clambering up out of the water. "You made me lose my fish."

"You stood too near the water. It was your fault."

"Catch my pole," shouted Nick. But it was too late. The pole, with its precious hook, drifted into the current and disappeared around the bend. Nick hated to lose the hook, but this was the first time any of the Indian children had played with him. He guessed that was worth a fishhook.

With only two poles, the turns at fishing went slower, while the pile of fish grew larger. The smaller children, hot and tired, took a fish or two and went home. The older kids raced around playing touch-tag when they weren't fishing.

"Brother, come in now," called M'lady, just as the sun dipped toward the western skyline. Nick trotted for home. He had a snug belonging feeling, that had been missing since he'd left Grantsville.

"Oops, I forgot my fish poles," he said aloud to himself. Back he went to the river. Most of the children were gone Nick picked up several fish and the unused pole that lay near the river. Patooli stood alone beside the water. Only Boni and Yagalont remained with her. They were in a contest of tossing their lariats at a stump.

"I need my fishing pole. I have to go in now." Nick grabbed at the pole Patooli held.

"Not now. It's my turn." Patooli jerked the pole from Nick's reach.

"I gotta go *now*," Nick said. He grasped the pole to yank it away from her. Patooli swung the pole at Nick, hitting him across the head. At that, she dropped the pole and ran. Nick reacted before he thought. He planted a kick squarely on her behind. He was sure he hadn't hurt her *that* much, but she screamed all the way home.

"I'm sorry I'm late," Nick told M'lady as he ducked into the tepee. He dumped his fishing poles and a few fish in a pile on the dirt-packed floor of the tent. "Those kids took my poles and most of the fish. I had to get them back."

"Let me at the white devil! Pocatello says true. You can never trust a white man." Patooli's mother burst into M'lady's tepee, a long knife clutched in her hand.

"You leave my tepee and my son to me. I will take care of them." M'lady stepped in front of Nick and shoved the other woman back outside.

Patooli's mother slashed out with her long knife. Blood sprayed from M'lady's head. "Stop it! You're killing my mother!" Nick grabbed up a three-foot club from the pile of firewood he had gathered earlier He thumped Patooli's mother soundly across the back.

A woman who had come as a spectator was caught up in the excitement. She grabbed M'lady by the bloody hair and sent her spinning. Nick lunged at the woman with his club. He flailed left and right, hitting anyone who got in his way. The whole camp erupted into a scratching, biting, pounding mob of women and children. The private battle over a fishing pole had become a camp free-for-all.

Someone saw Nick bashing people around and yanked his club away. Nick dashed into the tepee for more supplies.

"You sons of bitches," he screamed. "If you don't get out of here and leave my mother alone, I'll make some good Indians out of you!"

He put an arrow to his bow and aimed directly at Patooli's mother's heart.

CHAPTER 7

Strong hands grasped Nick from behind, holding him fast.

"You do not want to do that," said a deep voice that Nick recognized as Toosnamp's. "Yes I do! They all need killing," Nick screamed with rage.

Toosnamp held Nick firmly across the chest with one big hand. With the other, he swiftly cut Nick's bowstring in half. "You are not needed here at this time." Toosnamp pushed him into the tepee, away from the battle.

Nick quivered with anger and excitement, but he obeyed. He stayed inside as he was told, but watched through the flap. Men rushed up from all parts of the camp. Within a few minutes, they had calmed the trouble and led the women and children back to their own firesides.

Carefully, Toosnamp examined the cut on M'lady's head. It had bled a lot but Toosnamp assured Nick that it was not as serious as it looked.

An uneasy truce reigned in the camp for days. M'lady kept Nick always at her side. Together, they stripped the meat from the elk to make jerky. Together, Nick and M'lady carried the wood to feed their smoky fire.

Once they had gathered more wood than they could carry in a single trip, Nick ran back alone to fetch the remaining armful. With wood piled up to his eyes, Nick failed to see trouble approaching.

"You are a squaw," yelled Boni. He and Mopi sped across Nick's path. Mopi shoved Nick off balance, then circled him, yelling. Finally, he delivered the worst insult. He spat in Nick's face.

Wood flew every direction. Nick threw down his load and chased after the fleeing boys.

"Ooo-wee, ooo-wee." The boys ran from Nick, laughing, yelping and leaping as they ran. Mopi clutched his bare bottom with both his hands, daring Nick to kick him.

"Brother!" The word crackled through the air. Nick stopped

short. Washakie rode into camp astride his large buckskin horse. "What is the problem here?"

"They called me a girl and spit on me," said Nick, looking at his dirty hands. "Look at me!" said Washakie sternly. "I saw what they did. You must not chase them. They are being bad. They only want to cause trouble for you." He stepped down from his horse and helped Nick collect his wood.

A camp council was held around the fire at Washakie's lodge that night. Nick was not allowed to sit with the rest of the tribe, but from his bed within the tent, he could plainly hear.

"That white boy is a troublemaker," a voice said. "He kicks everyone he sees. He is causing problems for all of us."

Nick felt his face burning. He didn't mean to be a troublemaker. He didn't want to hear what else they said about him. But Washakie's voice boomed loudly.

"Has anyone ever seen the boy fight when someone did not provoke him?"

"I have watched him from the beginning, before I brought him to be with us. He is not quarrelsome, but he battles anyone who causes him trouble, as any one of us would do. He does not ask for special privileges," Toosnamp's voice answered. Nick felt better now, knowing that everyone didn't hate him.

"We do not like the way he does the work of the women. It will make our women want the other boys to do that, too."

"We burden our women to death with hard labor," Nick heard Washakie's voice again. "I did not think much about it until Little Brother came. I see how he helps Mother and how much hard work she has to do. Brother appears to be happier helping Mother than when he is playing all the time.

"I believe my mother would have gone crazy with sorrow if Brother had not come. Her sorrow for my father and my small brother was so much. I do believe the Great Spirit sent the little white boy to her."

54

"We do not want to live in the same camp with a white child."

Here it comes. Now they will sell me to the Sioux.

Instead, he heard Washakie say, "That is your choice. It is only three days' travel for you to go to the band of Hamori. You may go at sunrise."

Nick didn't see them go, but when the camp packed up to travel the next day, Patooli and her family were gone. When he questioned M'lady, she told Nick that three families had gone to Hamori's camp.

I wish none of this had ever happened, thought Nick. Back home it had been fun to pretend that he was an Indian. When he had played with Pandy, they shot bows and arrows, and played 'Kill the White Man'. Now he lived in an Indian house, ate Indian food, and talked Indian talk all the time. But he didn't have any Indian friends anymore. In fact, he didn't have any friends at all. That day back at the river, he had hoped he would have some friends but no one had played with him since.

Dejectedly, he rode his pinto behind the packhorses that carried Washakie and M'lady's belongings. Directly in front of him was a tired old mare, dragging the tent poles from her packsaddle. Nick hung back to keep out of the dust caused by the dragging poles.

Over to his left he saw Raida. She rode her small black pony ahead of her family's horses. She looked at Nick now and then, staring with large dark eyes. She didn't cover her face and giggle anymore. Instead she almost glowered when she looked in his direction. Nick wondered if she was thinking he would kick her. He wouldn't. He had never kicked anyone who hadn't asked for it. Besides, he'd never meant to kick a girl.

The sun rose higher. Sweat poured off him, soaking his leather shirt. A burning, stinging pain radiated through his neck and jaw. Nick grabbed the huge back horsefly from where it clung, biting him under the chin. Impulsively, he threw it away from him. The fly caught itself in mid-air, and flew dizzily toward the old mare that dragged the tepee poles. There it settled itself. Nick watched it crawl about lazily.

He had forgotten about the fly when suddenly the old mare ahead of him went crazy. Kicking with her back legs, she whirled around and poked the little stallion. ahead of her in the flank. The stallion bucked and whinnied. Then he dashed straight through the middle of the pack-string.

M'lady who seemed to be dozing as she rode, responded instantly. She headed her own horse into the path of the bucking, thrashing stallion, who was stampeding with all her possessions. The stallion jumped sideways, into M'lady's horse, knocking the old woman and her horse to the ground. The stallion and the rest of the pack- string scattered. Nick watched, frozen in his place.

Raida smacked her pony and away she raced, to where M'lady lay crumpled beneath her horse. The girl jumped to the ground and knelt beside the woman.

"Quick!" Raida looked at Nick. "Go get Washakie."

"It's Mother," Nick said when he reached Washakie, "She's hurt bad. I think she's dead." Then Nick burst into tears.

"Make camp!" Washakie called to Toosnamp, and whipped his buckskin back along the moving caravan, to where his mother lay on the ground. Her horse, his leg broken, had been dragged and pushed from her body by the women and girls who clustered around. Raida sat with M'lady's head cradled in her lap. The packhorses that had caused the accident stood nearby with drooping heads.

"She still lives," Raida's mother told Washakie. "We have sent a girl for the medicine man."

"There is bad luck living in this camp," the wizened, dark little medicine man declared. "The woman has a broken right arm. It is hurt above her elbow. If it does not mend well, I shall be forced to cut it off. She also has broken ribs. I am surprised she is not dead. When she took that white boy to be her son, she insulted the ghosts of her ancestors. They are not happy. However, put her to bed in her

56

own bed. Choose a girl to care for her and feed her aspen bark tea."

The little man shook his necklace of bones over the injured woman. "That will protect her," he said. He grunted twice, then stomped away on knobby little legs.

The women erected the old woman's lodge before they went to make their own. Raida steeped the aspen bark tea prescribed by the little man bedecked in the feathers and bones of his profession.

Outside, Nick waited and worried. Others, older and wiser in the ways of healing, had work to do. But he could do nothing. He didn't think too much of those ghosts that weren't happy with him. He hoped the Indians weren't happy with them. Then heard a cough and a groan.

"She needs you," said Raida. She took hold of Nick's sleeve and led him to the old woman's side.

"Stay with me, Brother," M'lady said weakly. "Do not leave me."

"I'll be right here," Nick said gratefully.

In the days that followed, Raida cooked and kept the fire for M'lady. Nick moped about the tepee doing nothing. There was no place he could go. He felt he needed to be close by in case M'lady called for him.

He finally brought a willow from beside the stream. Sitting near the lodge, he fashioned a willow-whistle. He hadn't even thought of a whistle since he came to the Indians.

"You can use this," Nick told M'lady as he presented the green whistle to her. "You blow in the end like this, and I can hear you from all over camp. I will run very fast to come to you."

M'lady curled her lips into a faint smile. "You are a good boy, she said.

*

"Why are you the one to stay and keep this lodge?" Nick asked Raida as the two of them carried armloads of wood to the tepee.

"My mother said that because the old grandmother has no daughter, I should be the one to help her. Because I there when she

57

was hurt that makes me more caring. That is the way we do." She looked strangely at Nick. "Why did you decide to be an Indian?" It was Raida's turn to question him.

Nick thought a while. "Indians are free. They can do what they want. They can go where they want. My Pa wouldn't let me have a gun. But I can hunt with a bow and arrow. I would like to catch horses with a rope, the way the warriors do. Indians have a good time."

I think I am glad you decided to be a Shoshone," Raida said. "If you like, I will show you how to use a lasso."

"I would like that."

Nick had watched the warriors with their ropes. He wanted to do the things they did. Over and over, he tossed the whirling rope at a stump that stood beside the tepee. Again and again he missed.

"I will never be able to do it right," he said gloomily to Raida. "I don't have that Indian touch."

"Yes you do," she said. "You should not give up so soon. The boys have been doing this since they were babies. I am only a girl. If I can do it so can you. Washakie is watching to see if you do well."

*

"Brother has worked hard to use a rope," Washakie told his Mother one day, some weeks after she was injured. "It is time for him to go hunting with me. Raida will help you while he is gone."

"What if he gets hurt or killed?" M'lady objected. "I would die if he were not here."

"Nothing will happen to him," Washakie said. "The scouts have found five buffalo over in the valley, a drink of water away. We will be back before dark. Some of the other boys are going. If he lives with us, Brother must learn the way to hunt."

That ended the discussion. Not even M'lady went against Washakie.

It was a beautiful day, cool enough to hear each sound. The other boys galloped along, joking and laughing. But Nick remained silent.

He could scarcely believe his good fortune. This was the time he had looked forward to since he left home. This was a time he had feared would never come.

The men rode their horses at an easy gait, as they loped along for over an hour. Finally Mopi's father, who was the leader of the hunt, stopped his horse and held up his hand. Everyone gathered around.

"We want to kill three buffalo. I will slip up behind them when they are not looking at me and cut the tendons of their back legs. Then you may shoot them with your arrows until they are dead."

When everyone understood what would be done, they all rode on in silence. Once, Boni told a joke to the four boys who rode near him.

"Sh-sh-sh!" warned Mopi. "We are approaching the buffalo. We must not warn them or they will run."

He thinks that because his father is chief of the hunt, that puts him over the other boys, Nick thought resentfully. Boni and the other four became quiet at once. *They probably think so too.* Well, Nick knew he wasn't going to do anything to be a troublemaker. This was the first Indian thing he had been allowed to do.

*

When the hunters returned to camp with their kill that evening, Nick was a good tired all over. He had shot all his arrows at a big buffalo bull. When the arrows were removed from the carcass, Nick was proud that three of them were his.

As he was drifting off to sleep, Nick had a thought. "My bow is too small," he told Washakie from his bed of buffalo skins. "I can't shoot hard enough to really kill a buffalo. I can only sting them a little bit."

Washakie chuckled. "You go on one hunt and already you become an expert. But you shall have a larger bow."

"Thank you," Nick said. "Then I will go out and kill a whole herd of buffalo."

Washakie roared with laughter. "Of course," he said. "What else would a white man do?"

CHAPTER 8

Morogoni, the old chief, made Nick a fine bow, longer and stouter than the one he had brought from home. Toosnamp gave him eight arrows just right for his longer new bow. The hunting party made several more trips for buffalo. Nick went along whenever Washakie did. It was the most exciting two weeks Nick could ever remember.

The hair on the back of Nick's neck always prickled as he watched Mopi's father creep noiselessly to the heels of one monstrous beast after another. With his long sharp spear, Buffalo Slayer cut the tendons at the heels of each shaggy dark animal, dropping it to its haunches. There it bellowed furiously, helpless to get away. With his heart pounding in his chest, Nick galloped along with the men and boys. Around and around they circled, time after time, shooting their arrows into an injured buffalo, until its head sank to the ground. There, with rolling eyes and lolling tongue, it waited for the warrior who finally slit its throat to let the life-blood drain from its neck.

"We need a gun," Nick told Washakie. Nick was so tired his legs quivered when he pressed his knees into his pony's ribs.

The men, who had killed nine buffalo, rode toward home feeling exhausted. The women took their turn at the slain beasts, busying themselves with stripping the great amounts of meat from the bones.

"If we had a gun, we could kill three times as many buffalo in half the time. Then we wouldn't be so tired," Nick sighed.

"A firestick would be fine, but we only kill what we need for food and clothing. If we did differently, the Great Spirit would not be pleased. We would not be Real People. If we wasted them, he would take the animals away, and we would go hungry. Only white men kill more than they need and leave meat scattered over the ground," Washakie told Nick.

Nick remembered the Goshutes Indians from back home. They ate anything they could get their hands on. They must have displeased the "Great Spirit" sometime in the past, because the wild animals were scarce where they lived. When the poor hungry Goshutes weren't stealing food from the Mormons, they ate gophers or grasshoppers.

*

When Old Mother was well enough to travel, the Indians rode again to the north. The scouts killed elk, deer, antelope and occasionally a moose along the way. Sometimes a few buffalo wandered close to the caravan. Whenever they did, the men killed only one or two. They didn't want to stop longer than one day to prepare the meat.

The scarlet leaves of the ground grapes and the golden and pale green of the quaking aspens turned the surrounding hills to a rainbow. The time until the snowfall was getting short. Early one morning, Toosnamp came to Washakie's tepee.

"The braves who went to get the horses this morning tell us that we are missing seven horses," Toosnamp said. "The tracks show that they were driven away. The Crows must have paid us a visit in the night."

Nick grabbed his bow and arrows and his food bag as he ducked out the door.

"Come back," Old Mother said, catching hold of Nick's shirt. "Where are you going?"

"I have to get my pinto. I am not going to let a Crow steal her," Nick said.

"Your horse is still here. The horses that are missing were the unbroken ones that were feeding on the hill. One was mine, one belonged to Washakie, three were Old Morogoni's and two belonged to the father of the twins," said Toosnamp.

"Well, lets go get them back," said Nick.

Toosnamp shook his head. "They are miles away by now. They were taken many hours ago."

"It is for the War Chief to decide whether the whole camp should go chasing after trouble," said Washakie. "He has already sent a scouting party to discover if there are any Crows lurking along our path. We are still many days from our winter range. We will wait until the scouts return before we decide to seek a fight."

Nick waited impatiently. When the scouts returned, they had found nothing. There was no battle. Instead, the camp moved on following the northern route. No one mentioned the missing horses.

One day—though no one said so—Nick knew that they had reached the winter camping grounds. A settled feeling hung in the air. Snow had fallen two days before and melted. The horses clomped about the broad meadow covered with knee-high dry grass. Their hooves cut muddy tracks wherever they stepped. A cold wind blew in the night, freezing the soggy ground, proving that the Indians were right on schedule. But though the air was crisp and cool, the sun still shone bright.

There was plenty of deer and elk to be found whenever fresh meat was needed. The Indians ate the dried jerky and pemmican only when no fresh meat could be found. The winter might be long with much deep snow. They must conserve their supplies as long as possible.

One afternoon while they were hunting, Washakie examined Nick's pinto pony. Its ribs showed plainly through its spotted hide.

"You have been riding your pony for a long time, Brother. It needs a rest," Washakie said. "I have a grey horse that has been used for packing. It will let itself be caught. You may ride it while your pinto rests and grows strong."

Nick knew that no horse would ever be as good as his pinto, but the grey was a sturdy three-year-old. It soon responded to Nick rapidly becoming a choice riding horse.

"I am pleased with the way you have trained the horse I let you use," Washakie told Nick a few weeks later. "If you will train some colts for me, you may keep the grey for your own."

"I will," said Nick eagerly. "I will start today. Which ones do you want me to break?"

"Bring your grey horse and your lasso to the horse pasture. I will

63

show you the colts I want broken. These horses have never been used; they have not been caught before. They will not be so easy to train as the grey horse was," warned Washakie.

"I can do it," Nick said. "I will come as soon as I get wood for Mother."

"I will help you with the wood and the horses too," Old Mother told Nick.

"No. I can do it myself," Nick insisted.

Nick easily lassoed one of the unbroken colts that Washakie pointed out to him. The horse was not at all sure that it wanted to go where the rope around its neck was taking him. He bucked and pulled, but all that happened was that he choked himself.

"Hold on to him tightly, and I will help you tie him to the tree at the end of the pasture," Washakie told Nick. Washakie crowded his own horse into the wild one with the lasso on its neck. He pushed the horse close to the small aspen tree. There, Nick tied it securely.

"Let it stand today with no food or water. Tomorrow it will be ready to be led to water," Washakie said. The horse rolled its eyes and tossed its head up and down. It circled the tree until its nose was wrapped close to the tree. Nick thought that was a poor way to treat a good horse but Washakie was right. The next day, the horse was willing to let Nick lead it to water and then back to his tepee.

"I need my saddle," Nick said to Old Mother, who looked out of the tepee inquiringly.

"You had better ride that horse without a saddle at first," Old Mother said.

"Don't worry. I can ride it," said Nick. "Anyway, I can't stay on without a saddle."

"There is a way if you want to know it," the old woman told him. "But I can see that you will do it your way."

When Nick tried to toss the saddle to the back of the wary horse, it shook its head and stepped away. Nick struggled with the saddle until sweat trickled into his eyes.

"How am I going to ride this stupid critter if I can't saddle it?" he finally asked Raida, who had come to watch.

"If you tie a blanket over its head so that it cannot see you, it will stand still. Then you can put the saddle on it." Raida ran into the tepee and returned with a cotton trade blanket.

Nick fastened the blanket over the horse's head and was happy to discover that she was right. He quickly saddled and mounted the mustang.

"Let 'er go!" he yelled in true cowboy fashion.

Raida untied the horse and pulled the blanket from its head. The horse stood with its head down and its feet wide apart for about three seconds. Then it noticed that it was free. It spun away from the tepee. Jumping and bucking, it tried to rid itself of its unwelcome burden.

Many children had gathered by this time, waiting for the spectacle. They had been watching silently while Nick struggled to saddle the horse. Now they ran after him, cheering. Nick wasn't sure if they were cheering for him or the horse. Nick managed to stay astride the horse while it was going straight ahead. When it got to the small creek that flowed near the camp, the horse changed directions but Nick didn't.

Splash. Nick landed in the shallow water. His horse, bucking at the saddle that had turned to hang beneath his plunged and pitched its way toward open country.

When Nick, who was thoroughly soaked, found the runaway, it stood with its head in a serviceberry bush. The rope still dragged from its neck. Nick gathered up the broken pieces of his saddle where they had been scattered across the meadow.

When he gave the broken fragments to Old Mother, she did not say, "I told you." She didn't say "Why can't you be more responsible." She said, "It can be repaired."

She took the saddle from him and went into her tepee.

"I guess I can never break wild horses," Nick told Raida. "I can't stay on a wild horse even with a saddle. I don't know how I can ride without one."

"If you put a rope tightly around its chest, behind its front legs you can slip your fingers under the rope and hang on to it," Raida told Nick. "If Mopi and the other boys ride beside you and keep the horse away from the trees, you can do it. Ride the horse now while it is tired, then he won't buck so hard."

That sounded all right to Nick. He borrowed Old Mother's blanket again, and instructed the boys on horseback what to do. Nick was sure they only wanted to see him dumped onto the ground again, but at least they agreed to help.

Success. The tired horse hardly fought at all. Soon Nick was trotting it around, guiding it by tugging at its mane. Nick discovered that it was fun to break horses; almost as much fun as hunting. The boys who had hunted beside him, rode beside him, helping him to control the wild horses he rode. He was bucked off often. Maybe it was because he was smaller than most of the boys, or maybe because he had finally learned how to fall, Nick was never hurt much. The challenge of conquering the horses was worth the bruises. The boys from all over camp helped him as he worked to break the colts. But they still called him squaw, when he carried wood or water for Old Mother.

Washakie said, "Don't listen to them. They act like Dog Stealers, not Real People."

So Nick tried to ignore the teasing and continued to use the boys' help to break the colts. One day Boni, Mopi, and some of the other boys were helping Nick to keep the mustang he was breaking, out of the bushes. The girls were watching the fun.

"Why do you have that stick, Mopi?" Raida called to her twin brother, who rode close to Nick. She pointed to a long sharp stick that Mopi held.

"This is a whip," Mopi said. He tapped his horse lightly on the rump. "I want to be close to Yagaiki when his horse throws him to

66

the ground. The baby needs someone to care for him."

Nick felt his ears burning. That wasn't fair. His horse had bucked him off twice already, and he hadn't cried yet.

The horse was taming nicely. This morning, Nick had put the saddle, rebuilt by Old Mother, on its back. He had his lasso tied carefully to the saddle horn in case he might need it. Today, he expected to ride this mustang as if it were a seasoned horse.

Nick's horse gave little bucking jumps, catching Nick off balance. If it hadn't been for the saddle, he would have hit the ground. The horse jumped again, kicking its left leg smartly.

"Whoa." Nick tried to sooth the nervous horse. Something was bothering it. *Maybe a horse fly,* he thought, remembering Old Mother's accident. Then out of the corner of his eye, Nick spotted the problem.

"Hey, stop that before I knock your head off," Nick yelped.

Mopi jabbed Nick's horse in the flank with the long pointed stick—again.

"You bastard!" screamed Nick. He yanked the lasso from his saddle and threw it furiously at his tormentor. "Let's see you stay on your horse."

The lasso settled neatly around Mopi's neck. Nick maliciously gave the rope a quick jerk. The flighty horse Nick rode could stand no more. Off it dashed, dragging Mopi from his horse to the ground.

Oh Lord, thought Nick. Now I've done it.

Mopi lit on his feet, running, grasping the rope in both hands to keep from being choked to death. Nick tried to undo the rope he had fastened so securely to his saddle, but it wouldn't come loose. He wished he had a long sharp knife like the one Toosnamp wore.

Then Nick remembered. He *did* have a knife. He pulled the little pearl-handled penknife from the pouch on his belt. Agonizingly, one strand at a time, he cut the rope that dragged Mopi along. Just as the tired boy stumbled on a rock and went to his knees, the rope gave way in Nick's hands.

Free from Mopi's neck, Nick didn't waste any time. He urged his fleeing horse forward. If there had been a camp fight when he had kicked a girl's butt over a fishing pole, he wasn't going to wait to see the brawl that would follow what he had done this time.

CHAPTER 9

Nick sat on a fallen log in the forest. Somewhere out there in the clearing he knew that a lot of screaming was going on. Mopi's mother had threatened once before to cut his heart out, and this time she just might succeed. It had been a lot of fun being an Indian. Maybe it hadn't all been fun, but it had all been exciting; not dull and boring life his life in Grantsville.

Here, he was a wild Indian hunting wild game and breaking wild horses. Back at Grantsville, he either watched sheep that weren't going anywhere or pulled weeds that never stopped growing. Here, the sounds of people chattering and dogs barking filled his ears. Back there, except for an occasional bleat of a sheep, or chirp of a bird, the sound of old Carney's bell was his only proof that he was not totally alone like Adam before God created Eve.

Nick took the saddle from the back of the half-broken horse. The horse might as well eat, even if *he* probably never would again.

He had left his bow and arrows and food bag back at camp; and his tiny penknife wasn't nearly as useful as he had imagined. Well, he had his fishhooks. If he got hungry enough, he would find a stream with fish somewhere in this forest. Now, however, he was plain cold.

The trees cast long shadows and the breeze that blew beneath the trees chilled him through. Behind the log, where he sat, was a pile of dead leaves. Nick rolled off the log and burrowed down into the leaves. He wriggled around until the nest of leaves fit him well and then...

He awoke with a start. It was growing dusk and night sounds surrounded him. Quickly, he threw the saddle on his horse and left the shelter of the trees. The fracas should be over by now. If it wasn't—well he'd just have to take his chances.

The old woman paced back and forth before the tepee, peering toward the forest. When she spotted him, her worried expression turned to relief.

"I knew you would come," she said and hugged Nick hard. "I would die if you left me like that."

"I didn't want to start another camp fight. I didn't mean to hurt Mopi," Nick told her.

"The whole camp knows that Mopi provoked the horse. It was all his fault. Raida said so. The other children told how Mopi poked that wild horse to make it buck. But roping some one and dragging them by the neck is a very dangerous thing to do."

"I forgot that the rope was tied to the saddle. Will the council make me leave this camp, the way they did Patooli?" Nick asked seriously.

"No. They warned Mopi that you are not yet a Real Person," Old Mother assured him. "You do not know how to behave like a Shoshone."

"The heck!" Nick's temper blazed. "That boy is a spoiled brat. If he isn't the center of attention all the time, he takes it out on everyone else. I think he needs a real hard thrashing."

"Thrashing? What is that?"

"Thrashing is when Pa takes you behind the shed and smacks you on the behind with a long willow switch," said Nick. "It would surely improve Mopi's manners some."

"Thrashing is a thing that Real People would never do. Children are given to us by the Great Spirit to care for. The Great Spirit gave you to me. I could never thrash you. Eat quickly and go to bed. It is already dark."

Old Mother gave Nick another hug. Then she handed him a juicy brown bird on a stick, and dropped the door flap behind him.

Nothing was ever said about that incident again. Mopi wore a rag around his neck—a greasy old rag that some Indian had gotten from some white man. Nick guessed that he had hurt Mopi pretty badly. He almost wished that he had choked the little smarty clear to death. *Well,* he guessed, *not really.* But at least Mopi was better behaved.

*

70

One day, a small band of antelope drifted near the camp. The entire camp raced out to surround them. The little gold-colored creatures with their slender horns and necks dashed back and forward within the circle of people, trying to find a way to escape. Every child, every man and woman had a club or spear. They struck the graceful animals as they sped about in terror. Indians tightened the circle, getting closer and closer to the antelope until the poor little things sank to their knees and put their heads under the bushes and waited to die. The warriors with their long knives cut the throats of as many as they needed for food. The rest were let go. All around. blood spurted, red and warm. The smell of fear and death filled the air. Bile rose in Nick's throat, and turning away, he puked his breakfast onto the frosty ground.

The memory of the antelope slaughter haunted Nick. Hunting elk or deer was different. They always had a chance to flee, but these graceful little creatures were trapped in a circle of fear.

As the days grew shorter, the women worked furiously, filling leather bags with jerky and pemmican, a mixture of fish or meat and berries, ground into a pulp. The men, who had been collecting obsidian and chert all summer, poured their collections of stone on the ground. They then proceeded to repair or replace their broken or lost spears and arrows.

When Pocatello and his war party rode into camp one day Nick didn't run to meet them the way the other children did. He remembered when Pocatello's warrior had tried to capture him back at the council. Old Mother had made Nick all new clothes and he was dressed like the other boys. She had made him a hat of rabbit skins with a rabbit tail on top. It covered his hair. Washing was not Nick's favorite chore and now that no one made him, he didn't wash at all. His filthy hands were nearly as dark as the Indians'. He Supposed his face was too. But he still had those darned blue eyes. So he stayed way back, while the rest of the tribe clustered around the visitors.

"They were foolish. They could not have crossed the mountains before the snows came," Pocatello said to Washakie. He spoke loudly and everyone in the camp could hear.

"Three wagons were traveling alone. They did not know where we came from and they did not even fight back," a painted warrior boasted.

"We have many things to trade. We need pemmican and jerky to eat as we travel back to our camp. We will also trade for horses, buffalo robes or a saddle," said Pocatello. "We do not want to trade the scalps."

The visitors displayed some hair with red attached. They lifted the eight scalps high for all to see.

"I will trade a bag of obsidian for this," said one of Washakie's braves. He held up a man's coat, black with long tails and velvet lapels.

The whole camp began pawing through the pile of trade items on the ground in front of them. A quilt with a patchwork star in the middle, done in oranges and reds, was coveted by many of the women and the haggling for it was heated.

"See what I got for you," said Old Mother, obviously pleased with the large-brimmed grey felt hat she held out to Nick, when she found him lurking behind a tepee.

Nick grabbed it and flung it from him. "I can't wear that!" he shouted. "My pa has one just like it. The man who owned that hat is dead. Pocatello and his men killed all the people in those wagons. They rode their ponies in a circle around them and the people couldn't get away. They were trapped just like those little antelope were. Only, we didn't kill all the antelope, just what we needed food. But Pocatello didn't want to eat those people did he?"

Nick trembled in anger. He ran into the tepee and dropped the door flap. He wished he could have slammed it.

Pocatello and his warriors stayed as guests at Washakie's camp for three days. Nick was relieved when they moved on, their faces cleaned from the war paint they wore when they had arrived. He knew that somewhere out in the mountains were the burned remains of three wagons and some poor, unburied people. Without the warriors and their scalps to remind him, Nick hurriedly put the thoughts from his mind.

*

It was a long autumn. The snow fell like hoarfrost to melt in the first rays of the sun. Then, as if to tell winter not to hurry, the weather grew warmer again and the children played frantically in the shortening days. Nick played as hard as any, running, shooting, and roping anything he saw, to fill the daylight hours.

Once he was so caught up in the games that he didn't hear the first time Old Mother called him. When he did hear, he decided that he wasn't ready to go in. He ignored her and kept on with his game. He raced among the trees at the edge of the clearing. There she stood in front of him. He turned to run and Old Mother grabbed his shirt at the back of the neck.

"Why didn't you come when I called?" Old Mother demanded.

Nick struggled to free himself and succeeded only in tightening the front of his buckskin shirt across his windpipe.

"Wait! Wait a minute! I can't breathe!"

"You come now!" Old Mother jerked him along toward their tepee.

"Please let me go. I'll come. I promise," Nick begged.

She pushed him angrily through the door flap, shoving him at a pile of sleeping robes. Nick, waving his arms for balance, missed the pile and lit with a thud on the hard packed floor. Washakie, who sat nearby attaching a metal point to an arrow, reached out to steady Nick.

"Why didn't you come when I called?" Old Mother again demanded. "You were right there. I could see you." Her voice shook with rage and Nick knew that she would start to bawl any second now.

"I wanted to play." Nick ducked his head. "The other boys are still outside. I shoot as good as any of them. I have just as many scalps." Nick pulled a handful of twigs and dried leaves from the leather thong that he had knotted about his middle, and threw them furiously at her feet.

A cloud of pain flickered across Old Mother's face. "Washakie," she said as she left the wigwam. "You must do something about this boy. He will not mind *me*."

Outside, she made that noise women make. Loud and long. "Ooo-wee ooo-wee Ooo-wee."

Well, let her bawl. If she doesn't care about me, why should I care about her? He clenched his hands into fists and stared at them.

"What is wrong between you and Mother?" Washakie asked.

"I hate to be treated like a baby," Nick answered without looking up. "Every night when the sun goes down she starts. 'Brother do this... Brother do that... Brother, come in... Brother, go to bed!' The other boys play after dark. Why can't I?"

Washakie thought a while. "Mother knows," he said finally. "Why don't you ask her? You should be good to her and mind her. She is good to you. Better than she ever was to me."

As if she had been listening and waiting for the right moment, Old Mother poked her head back into the tepee. The red blanket that had been about her shoulders now covered her grey hair.

"Brother, you make me afraid." She spoke so low that Nick had to lean toward her to hear. "When it is dark, evil things might happen and no one would know. I want you to be safe. I want you inside with me."

"But we don't do evil things," Nick said, pleading with her. "We only play 'Kill the White Man.' When we shoot the leaves off a branch, we call it a scalp. Whoever gets the most scalps gets to be War Chief. I had just as many as anyone. Maybe I would have been the chief."

"Oh you foolish child." Old Mother knelt in front of him. "All their lives, those boys have been playing 'Kill the White Man'. Don't you know? *You* are the White Man. Any of them would be glad to take your scalp if they thought that no one would see.

"You're wrong!" said Nick emphatically. "We are only playing. I am their friend."

"Ha!" Old Mother said loudly. "You have kicked them in the belly. You have fought with them over a fish pole. You have dragged them from their horses with a rope around their necks. I don't think you are much of a friend."

Nick felt his face grow hot under the layers of dirt. He didn't like to remember the camp fights his actions had caused.

"They always started things," he muttered. Then he expertly turned the focus from his misdeeds. "Do you really think they would scalp me?"

Old Mother ran her fingers through Nick's tangled curls. "Yes. They would scalp you. Just like Pocatello attacks every wagon train and scalps every white man he can. You may dress like an Indian, you may ride and shoot like an Indian. But you have a white man's scalp. If you want to keep it, you had better not forget that."

CHAPTER 10

Winter finally came with a rush. A heavy, wet snow dropped in the night. When Nick looked out through the flap one morning, the snow lay sparkling in a beautiful field of white. It bent low the evergreen branches above his head.

The dogs, tails curled around their noses, rolled into furry balls against the walls of the tepees to collect whatever heat escaped. There wasn't much.

Strange people, these Shoshones, Nick thought. *They prepare food to last all winter but totally ignore their fuel.* The dry sticks that had lain on the ground in plentiful supply the day before were now buried under eighteen inches of snow.

Old Mother was a marvel in the camp. The aches and pains in her bones had warned her of the approaching storm. With Nick's help, she had gathered enough firewood to last through the storm. Some of the women had followed her example and collected firewood also. Most of the tepees, however, had lost their fire completely.

The women with papooses in their homes mustered their courage, wrapped their feet in squares of leather tied over their moccasins, and threw a trade blankets over their heads. They trudged out into the knee-deep snow and up into the foothills. Using the same stone hammers or axes that their ancestors had used, they gathered the branches from dead trees; anything to keep their fires going.

Not many, however, cared to brave the cold. Most of the camp followed the example of the dogs. They rolled up in the sleeping robes and encouraged the children to do the same.

Nick couldn't be kept inside. Snow was his element. He plopped into an unblemished patch of white and swung his arms and legs in wide arcs, whooping delightedly. When he stood to brush the snow from his clothing, he smiled in satisfaction. His snow angel was as beautiful as it had ever been in Grantsville.

Soon other youngsters, curious as to his joyous shouts, joined Nick to roll and play in the snow. It was not long before snowmen stood about guarding snow forts, while snowballs whizzed through the air. The first snowfall of the year was especially for children. Finally, wet and cold, Nick returned to his tepee.

"It sure isn't very warm in here," he complained. "Why don't you pile more wood on the fire and make it warm?"

"Wood is not easy to get when the snow is deep," said Old Mother. "This wood may have to last for many days."

"Well, let's go get some more," said Nick logically. "There is a lot of wood up in the foothills."

"That is a long way to carry it," said Old Mother. "Anyway, an armful does not last very long."

"Let's get a whole bunch," said Nick. "We can do that."

"If you want to spend all day every day carrying wood, you may do so," said Old Mother. "I have hides to tan and clothes to make. I do not have time to gather wood to burn in a big hot fire."

"All right then, I will," Nick said.

He remembered the sled he had watched Pa make to fetch wood from the woodpile to the house. It had been a little hand sled, but Nick had grander ideas. In a grove of quaking aspen about a half-mile from camp he found what he wanted. He selected two small dead trees with a curve at one end where the trees had bent to grow straight up the hillside. The trunks of these trees would make perfect runners. With the auger he had carried in the pouch he wore at his belt since he had left Grantsville, Nick made holes through the runners. He then used rawhide strings to tie short poles across the runners. This made a proper sled close to the ground.

Nick borrowed two of Old Mother's gentlest packhorses. By fastening the sled to their packsaddles with ropes, they were able to pull the sled. Nick piled the sled full of small dead trees for firewood. Riding one of the horses to guide and control the sled, he took the wood to camp. In three days, he had enough wood to last

78

Old Mother the rest of the winter.

"Will you let us use your mighty machine?" asked three of the younger men, when they saw the pile of wood Nick had gathered.

"The white man has clever ways to do things. Our women are tired of gathering wood."

"Sure," Nick agreed. It wasn't often he could teach them anything. He watched them go, laughing and shouting, a man on each horse, and one on the sled. They didn't stop at the grove of trees on the foothills where Nick had gathered his wood. They kept going until they were on the steep slope of the mountain.

That's too high, Nick thought to himself, but he was too far away to call to them. He went to play with the other children and soon forgot about the wood gatherers.

In the early afternoon, Nick heard them coming back. Their whoops and chants sounded as if a whole war party was attacking the camp. The pile of poles on the sled was as high as the horses' backs. All three of the men had seated themselves on top of the load of wood, leaving the horses with no one to guide them. The sled dragged heavily through the deep snow until they came to the place where Nick, with his wood getting, had packed down a trail. The horses picked up a little speed. So did the sled, piled high with wood.

Nick watched, aghast. He knew they were headed for disaster. The sled ran into the rear of the horses' legs and they started to run. Faster and faster went the horses. Faster and faster went the sled, bumping the horses at every step. Soon they were in a frenzy. Straight through the village of tepees they dashed. When the men saw where they were headed, they jumped off the sled into the snow. The horses, dragging the wood with them, knocked over tepees all along their trail. Wood and sled were scattered throughout the camp.

Washakie and Toosnamp caught the frightened horses, to return them to their owners.

"The white man builds dangerous contraptions," said one of the men. He picked himself out of the snow and took the horses from

79

Washakie.

"Getting wood is woman's work," said another. He solemnly brushed the snow from his buckskin leggings.

"If we do all the women's work, they will not have anything to do to keep them happy." The third man joined his companions in making excuses for themselves.

"One small boy did more than three grown men, said Toosnamp. "He can make the horses and the snow work for him. All the men can do is make their wives do their work."

Washakie suppressed a smile. "Brother," he called. Come and gather up this sled that is scattered all through the camp."

It wasn't hard for Nick to patch up the broken sled. Most of it lay in a jumble by the largest pile of wood. He repaired the broken crosspieces and hitched his creation to the packhorses again. He felt bad about the damage his sled had done, so to salve his guilty conscience he gathered wood for the entire camp.

"Let's have some fun," Nick said to the boys who had helped him unload the last of the wood.

Nick led Old Mother's gentlest horse with his sled to the top of hill while the boys trooped behind, eager to see the 'fun'.

"Come on with me, somebody. Let's take a ride," Nick said when he had the sled perched on the edge of the slope, ready for the downward plunge.

"We are not foolish," said Mopi, backing away. "We saw what that machine did to the warriors."

"We aren't going to do it that way," said Nick. "We won't be tied to the horse so it can run away with us."

"I will ride with you if some one else will go also," Raida said. As usual she had followed the boys. She turned to her brother. "Mopi, you come with me."

"Not me, said Mopi." Gowani will ride with you." He pushed the small boy toward the sled.

"Now you push us off the hill; then bring the horse to where we stop at the bottom, to pull the sled up again." Nick loosed the horse, settled himself on the sled and motioned Raida and Gowani to climb on behind him.

"Here we go!" whooped Nick as down the hill they swooped.

"Not Gowani," said Raida in his ear. "He jumped off back where we started."

"That's all right. Get ready now. When I say to lean, you do what I do and we will have a fine ride," Nick yelled over his shoulder.

Nick and Raida sped toward the tepees at the bottom of the hill. Raida clung tightly and Nick felt a shudder shake her shoulders. She must be scared.

"Lean now!" he screamed. He bent his body to the right, and Raida, hanging on in desperation, leaned too. The sled curved in a wide arc and swept across the flat ground, away from the village until it slowed and glided to a stop.

"That was a fine ride. We flew like a bird—an eagle, I think," Raida told the boys when they puffed through the snow, leading the old horse. Nick tied the horse to the sled again and away they went up the hill.

"I will stay on that thing this time," Gowani assured Nick. "I will take my turn now."

"Boni will ride with me this time," Mopi said. "If Gowani is going to ride, he must get on the back."

"There is room for more than that," said Nick. Pile on, everybody who can hang on. That will make it more fun."

When they heard that, six boys climbed on behind Nick. Down and up, down and up. Raida rode the horse to the bottom of the hill and Nick rode it back up again, pulling Raida behind it. Dragging the sled to the top of the hill and swooping down again with a pack of children behind him, filled Nick's days and weeks. The little ones, the big ones, boys and girls, all the children in the camp, waited their turns to load onto the sled and drop off the hillside with their stomachs in their throats.

81

The women had more than once threatened Nick's life. He did not believe that they would take it kindly if the sled should run amok and plow through their homes again. He was sure that none of the other boys understood the mechanics of steering the crude sled away from the village. He realized he had created a monster. Each morning all the children huddled at the top of the hill waiting for him to arrive with his sled.

When he awoke to hear wind whistling and snow pelting the elk-skin tent, one morning, Nick sighed with relief—no sledding today. The storm blustered on through the whole week. Slyly, one stick at a time, Nick dismantled his terrible, wonderful contraption and sneaked it inside the tepee to feed the smoky fire. That sled must have made a million trips up and down the hill. The runners were nearly worn out and Nick had been with the sled on every trip it made.

When the blizzard blew itself away and the other boys asked about the sled, all Nick said was, "It's gone," and not one person asked "Where?"

Being with the Indian children every day, all day, playing with the sled had created a bond between Nick and the tribe that had not existed before. The grown-ups told each other of the men who had torn up the tepees on their excursion after wood, and laughed. They smiled at Nick and reached out to pat him on his shoulder. He felt that he was now a Shoshone. But Old Mother still wanted him the wigwam by sundown.

*

Suddenly it was spring. The snows melted and the mud dried up. A green shadow crept over the trees and the ground. The willows and the bare rosebushes along the creek turned from dull grey to brilliant red overnight. The aspen grove on the hillside grew golden to the tips of their leafless twigs. In the horse pasture, wobbly colts in spotted coats gamboled on their spindly legs. An urgency to be alive sprang into Nick's being. Wrestling, racing and killing the white man became favorite games again. The whole Indian camp seemed to be marking time, waiting to move, while the horses grew fatter.

On the other side of the horse pasture was a river of rocks, tumbling down the mountainside. Boulders and pebbles and rocks of every size began rolling somewhere up on the mountain and spilled down its face. This was a fascinating place. The children raced each other to see who climb the highest upon the rocks.

"See me. I am the highest chief in the whole Shoshone Nation," Yagamont crowed from his lofty perch atop a boulder halfway up the mountainside.

"Look out below. We are going to send a mighty attack on our enemies." Boni and Mopi combined their efforts behind a large boulder and pushed. The rock didn't budge. It was more than two boys could handle.

"Come and help us," they called to anyone who was near. Nick and Gowani climbed to their assistance.

"You had better be careful," Raida called up the hill toward them. "Someone might get hurt if you aren't careful."

"Well then, get out of the way," Mopi told her. The boys pushed and shoved, shoulder to shoulder until the boulder was began to move. Down it rolled, slowly at first, then as it gathered speed, smaller rocks along its trail dislodged to tumble with it. The boulders leaped and bounced, jumping high into the air to come down on rocks lower down the hill, which in turn knocked other rocks loose as well.

The rumble echoed through the valley. A curious yearling colt, who had been standing too near, watching, turned to run, but the rocks came too fast. A large flying rock struck it in the middle of the back and it fell to the ground, whinnying in pain. Warriors rushed to the pasture in time to see the last trickle of rocks descending.

"You are foolish to do such a thing," Mopi's father scolded them as the children climbed cautiously down the rocks to the ground. "The whole mountainside might begin to move and bury all of you

83

in a tomb of boulders."

When he saw that the pony had suffered a broken back, he quickly cut its throat to end its pain.

"There will be no more rolling of rocks," said Washakie. "Go back to your lodges now so that your mothers will see that you have not been injured."

That night, they ate the pony for supper. The boys stayed away from the mountainside for a day or two, but the lure of the rocks drew them like a magnetic force. In the short time the children had been gone, a remarkable thing had happened. Now climbing on the rocks in the same way the children had, were dark brown furry animals. Nick had never seen anything like them. The animals resembled bears but they were no larger than a jackrabbit or a porcupine. They stood on hind legs with their little front feet suspended in the air. They didn't seem to have any fear of the children. Curiously, they stood watching as the children approached. But when the children got too close, all the animals ducked from sight.

"The rock chucks are back," shouted Boni. "Now we can have a a feast. Let's go get our bows and get some.

"We were told not to come here," Raida said.

"Oh no," Mopi assured her. "Washakie said don't roll rocks. He didn't say don't shoot whistle-pigs. I am going to get my bow and kill me one for supper."

The boys were eager to follow Mopi's example. Although Nick didn't waste any time going or coming, several children were already there when he reached the hillside with his weapon.

The boys ranged around the bottom of the rock mountain taking aim at the plump brown varmints. Nick took aim and let his arrow fly at the pot-bellied brown target. As if by magic, the rock chuck vanished.

"Did you hit one?" asked Gowani.

"Not me," said Yagamont. "Nobody did."

"They are clever," said Gowani. He laughed gleefully, as if he thought that the rock chucks had played a huge joke on them all. "I think I can shoot one if I am careful."

Gowani ran a little closer and ducked behind a large boulder that had rolled to the pasture floor, when they had rolled the rocks a few days before.

"Let me show you why they are called whistle-pigs," Mopi said to Nick. He gave a shrill whistle and all across the mountainside, little brown heads with round staring eyes popped up among the rocks.

"They are funny," said Raida. "They look like tiny people who want to see why you called them."

"I got one!" called Gowani, from his hiding place behind the boulder. Nick glanced at Gowani. The rock chuck he had been watching was gone when he looked back to where it had been.

"Whistle again," Nick told Mopi. "When they poke their heads up, we will be ready for them."

"Be very quiet. We might scare them," Raida cautioned. She placed her arrow in her bow with great care.

Excited boys waiting at the foot of the rockslide placed their arrows in their bows and drew back. Again, a piercing whistle ricocheted among the rocks. Brown fuzzy creatures bounced into sight across the face of the rock-strewn hill. Nick paid no attention to Gowani as he climbed up the rocks to retrieve his trophy. When the whistle echoed up the rock hillside, Gowani stood erect. Grinning, he waved at his comrades.

Two-dozen boys and one girl each let fly an arrow at the rock pile and laughed delightedly to see the targets drop from sight.

One little boy screamed in pain and pitched head first onto a rock, dislodging it. Down the hill he tumbled; the rock tumbled with him. Other rocks set in motion also began to descend.

"Oh God!" Nick screamed, as the sight before him registered in his brain. Gowani lay across a rock near the bottom of the hillside

85

and he didn't move at all.

CHAPTER 11

Nick clamped his hands over his ears, trying to shut out the sounds. He missed Gowani as much as anyone did, except maybe Gowani's mother or father. Gowani had always been a nervy little fellow. He would try anything. Nick shuddered. All this yelling and bawling was making him crazy.

"If you do not mourn with the rest of the tribe, people will think you are a cruel boy who cares only for himself," Old Mother said. "Now cry loud and show the proper respect."

Nick did. He cried and howled as loud and as long as he could. But this had been going on for five days now, for heaven's sake. How much crying could a fellow do? He would be glad when the whole thing was over and done with.

When Gowani had fallen down the mountain. and everyone had rushed to where he lay sprawled on the rocks, Nick was relieved that the arrow that had gone through Gowani's windpipe was not his.

Raida had run back to camp to tell the women about the accident. Nick had held one of Gowani's arms. Yagamont had lifted him by the other one. Mopi and Boni carried Gowani by his legs. They had almost reached camp when Gowani's mother dashed out ahead of the other women. She made them put him down while she put her hand on his heart. When she was sure that he was really dead, she took her son in her arms and carried him all the way back to her lodge. There she sat down beside her tent and held Gowani in her lap. She rocked him and cried for the rest of the day.

When the men got back from their elk hunting trip, Gowani's father put streaks of white paint across his nose. He painted black lines from his eyes to his chin. Nick thought that it looked as if Gowani's father had been crying black tears that ran down his face and dripped off his chin. After he had his face painted just right, Gowani's father went to the rock mountain. There he found a hole that was deep enough. He returned to the boy's mother, who still held Gowani's lifeless body. She cried and moaned, rocking back and forth.

"We must bury him now so that he can go be with the Great Spirit," he told her gently.

Nick had never seen an Indian burial. He had watched with morbid interest as Gowani's father laid a buffalo robe on the ground. Carefully, Gowani's body was put on the robe. Gowani's mother cut off her long braids and placed them on Gowani's chest.

The whole camp then marched past the body on the buffalo robe. Some put little gifts beside him: a pouch of food, an arrow, a pair of moccasins.

"Isn't that a waste of good moccasins?" Nick asked Old Mother. "Why don't they give them to Gowani's little brother? They would almost fit him now."

"Gowani was an oldest son. No one can ever walk in his moccasins. Besides he will need them for his long journey. See how great his mother's mourning is. She put her beautiful hair into his blanket. When Gowani meets the Great Spirit, he can show that he is an oldest son and much loved. Follow me and tell him how much you will miss him."

Nick and Old Mother got into line and marched by the buffalo robe.

"Have a speedy trip."

"You will be in my thoughts."

"You will be missed."

"Here is an arrow to insure your protection."

One after another, the people ahead of Nick placed their hands on Gowani's head and gave the lifeless body a parting message or a gift.

Nick had never touched a dead person and he didn't intend to do it now. When they had carried Gowani with the blood dripping from his throat, Nick hadn't thought of him as dead—so that didn't count.

"You must," Old Mother said. "You do not want to make me ashamed."

So Nick finally put his hand on the waxy, cold head. "I am sorry you are dead," he muttered, and quickly moved away.

Gowani's family tied his little body to the back of his pony. The whole camp moved in a procession to the rock mountain. There his father tucked the body wrapped in the buffalo robe into the hole that had been found. He then cut the pony's throat. As its lifeblood streamed over the rocks, Gowani's father led it close to the hole and pushed it in, too. The whole tribe, then, set to work. They tossed in rocks of various sizes to cover the boy and his horse.

"I don't understand," said Nick. "If they didn't want that horse, they could have given it to me. I could always use another horse."

"Hush, you bad boy," Old Mother told him. "Would you have the oldest son of a Shoshone warrior walking to the Great Spirit, like a Goshute or a Paiute? The Great Spirit would never know that Gowani belonged to the Real People. Now you must do your duty to his parents. Cry!"

Now, Nick sat inside Old Mother's tepee. The moaning and howling rose around the entire camp, in a high keening wail.

"Owee-oweee—aii-aiii-aii."

Even with his hands on his ears, Nick could not keep out the sounds. He thought back to when his baby sister had died. Ma had wrapped the baby in her Sunday silk shawl with the long shiny fringes all around. Pa had nailed her little body into the wooden box that had held Ma's good dishes when they traveled across the plains. Pa dug a hole down by Overlook Rock, and buried the box.

Nobody was there but Pa and Ma and Sylvester and him. Nobody cried. He wished they would have because he wanted to cry, but he couldn't cry alone. Pa had said that men don't cry.

Ma had turned her back to the little mound of dirt and walked stiffly back to the cabin. Her eyes looked red and hot. She wrapped her empty arms around her thin body as if she was trying to feel the tiny girl that she had held close the day before. Ma never mentioned the baby again. But she went about with a distant look in her eyes as if she was remembering.

Nick wondered if Ma had that look in her eyes for him. He wished he knew if she thought of him now or wondered if he was alive.

Well, it was too late to think about that now. He was an Indian boy, the brother of the chief. He got up from where he sat and went back outside. All the anguish of his heart spilled over. He joined the rest of the tribe and wailed away his sorrow.

*

When Nick awoke the next morning, change was in the air. Enough time had passed in mourning. Now, men were talking and laughing.

"Get up," Old Mother said. "We must move. This camp is a place of death. The deer and elk will no longer come here to eat. Now we must move to where they are."

Within a short time, they were on the trail again. Washakie spoke to Old Mother, and Nick was allowed to ride with the men. Hanabi, the young woman who had been walking about with Washakie, took Nick's place. She helped Old Mother with the packhorses. She had a slim waist and a smile in her soft brown eyes. Nick thought that she liked him as much as she liked Washakie.

As the days passed into weeks, they traveled uneventfully southward, through meadows blooming with purple and yellow spring flowers. The fragrance of the wild roses mingled with the dust. Nick had forgotten the sorrow of so short a time before. He was filled with a glowing glad feeling that poured from him onto everything he saw. *This is what happy means,* he thought. He hoped nothing ever changed.

Washakie finally signaled a stop. The trees, aspen and evergreen, skirted the clearing. The stream meandering nearby was edged with tall reeds bearing last year's ragged cattails. Soon the horses were wearing their leather thong hobbles around their front ankles. With tiny dancing steps, they spread out across the meadow to feed. Then Nick and the other boys were free to explore.

Somewhere in that wide clearing there must be something to shoot. A colony of watching chipmunks with cunning dark stripes down their furry grey backs disappeared beneath the ground when the boys approached.

"You make too much noise," Yagamont complained to Mopi.

"Not me," said Mopi. "I am as silent as a hawk. Everyone knows that hawks are noiseless hunters."

"Look!" Nick pointed at a half-grown black bear. Its fur looked dry and dusty. Large hairless spots showed on its side and back. The bear looked back over its shoulder at the children but didn't slow its pace. It crashed through the dead limbs of a fallen tree and loped toward the stream.

"We can get him!" Nick said eagerly. He lifted his bow from his shoulder. "He is big enough. We can all shoot him! If he runs, we can chase him and kill him."

"Oh no," said Boni. "We can not kill the bear. Its skin is thicker than a buffalo. If we try to hunt him, he will kill us. He is hungry. He could eat all of us in one bite if he wanted to."

"He wants to fish," said Mopi. "We should let him fish."

"I think you are all afraid," said Nick. "We could get him if we all get together. He wouldn't know what to do if we all shot him."

"It is too skinny. It would not taste good," said Raida. "If you try to shoot it, I will tell. We have been told to leave the bears alone."

Nick didn't argue anymore. He knew it would do no good. He could not kill the bear by himself. And if Raida told, Old Mother might haul him back into the tepee. Then he would not be able to play at all.

"These Indians think they are so brave," he said to Washakie and Old Mother that night. "But if anything might fight back, they run like scared deer. I think they are a bunch of cowards. If my Pa saw a bear, he would shoot it in a minute."

"You must be cautious when you see a bear," said Washakie.

"Bears are mean," Old Mother added. "The Great Spirit sends

the souls of murderers to live in them. Bears love to kill Real People."

Washakie smiled at his mother's old legend. "It is wise not to cross trails with them, Brother. They are strong. They could catch you and eat you before you could run away. As Mother said, bears are mean."

*

The days passed. The horses grew fat. Old Mother took Hanabi under her care. Even though he was a little bit jealous, Nick was also glad. Old Mother let him roam farther away from the tepee, and she let him go with Washakie when he went hunting.

On one trip, Washakie shot a large bull elk. The elk fell heavily to the ground. "It will soon be dead," Washakie told Nick. "When the elk no longer moves, cut its throat beneath its chin and let the blood drain out. That will make the meat much better. We will give its skin to Hanabi to make the white dress she wants so much."

Washakie took his long knife from its scabbard and handed it to Nick. "I will return to camp and bring back a horse. Also we will need someone to help us load it on the horse. It is much too big for you and me to lift."

Nick looked at the large animal, with its kicking legs and thrashing head. "Don't you think we should shoot it again to make sure it doesn't run away?"

"Oh no. That would make more holes in its skin. Hanabi needs a perfect skin for her dress. That old grandfather will die soon. You must have a small amount of patience." Washakie walked away with long purposeful strides.

Indians are as foolish as anybody else when they fall in love, thought Nick.

Nick watched while the huge elk struggled to rise. He was glad that it didn't make it. . But it turned its large head and looked straight at him. *I had better go back into the forest so it can't see me,* thought Nick. *If it gets to its feet, it might come and knock me down and stomp on me. I couldn't even shoot it again because Washakie doesn't want me to make any more holes in its skin.*

Nick slipped cautiously back into the trees. When he looked again at the place where the elk had lain in the tall grass, he could see nothing. *Maybe it is dead,* he thought. *No, I bet it has gotten up and is looking for me.* So Nick ran further back into the thicket.

He waited a long time. Washakie didn't come and that mean old elk was somewhere in that forest looking for him. Maybe if he climbed a tall tree he could see the elk. Or if Washakie was coming, he might see him. The only problem was that the really tall pines didn't have any branches close to the ground. Their branches started about fifteen feet in the air. Oh well, he'd look around until he found a tree he *could* climb.

Finally, Nick went back toward what he thought was the clearing where he had left the elk. Somehow, everything looked different. He didn't remember that big cottonwood tree. Nick climbed the cottonwood and looked around. He couldn't see the place where the elk had fallen. Trails crisscrossed the clearing. Except for the black and white magpies chattering in the trees, the world was silent.

Nick slid back down the tree and sat with his back resting against it to wait. The sun warmed him and the flies buzzed around his sweating face. He couldn't imagine why Washakie didn't come. Across the clearing something moved. That wasn't the elk that was barely visible over the grass.

Nick watched soundlessly. He didn't move a muscle. Was lt what he thought it was? Yes! There could be no doubt. There were three Indian warriors creeping across the far side of t he clearing. By the blue war paint across their noses and the black feathers tied to their left arms, Nick could tell they were not from Washakie's tribe. They didn't look in his direction.

Nick waited until he could no longer see the warriors. Then crawling slowly, he made his way to where the three men had disappeared into the timber. Once inside the forest, they hadn't bothered to hide their tracks. The footprints were plain in the moist, mossy ground beneath the trees. A short way back into the thicket, Nick could see where they had tied their horses. Piles of horse dung were steaming where the horses had stood. The men had obviously mounted the horses and were moving slowly, single file through the timber. They had enough of a start on him that Nick didn't worry about being seen. Suddenly, Nick nearly stumbled into the horses. They were well hidden in the underbrush. He was close enough so that he could have reached out and touched one of them on the rump. The horses whickered softly. Nick gulped and released his breath, relieved the Indians were no longer with their mounts.

Carefully, so that he wouldn't snap a twig or rustle a leaf, Nick threaded his way forward. *Easy now—there they are.*

The men lay flat on their stomachs and peered through the undergrowth at the edge of another clearing. Keeping trees to the north of him, between himself and the warriors, Nick inched forward to see what they were looking at. In the clearing, horses were grazing. At the far end of a meadow, near a stream, was a village of wigwams. Children and dogs romped about. They were at least a half-mile away. Nick could only faintly hear the barking of the dogs. He felt dangerously close to those invaders crouching in the grass.

Good Lord! thought Nick. That's our camp! These Indians, whoever they are, are checking out our horse pasture. They are going to steal our horses, and if they see me, they will steal me, too. It was a long way across the clearing to where his Indians were going about their business so unsuspectingly.

To the south of him, inside the forest, Nick heard more horses. He heard a man's voice so quiet that he couldn't tell what it said. They had him surrounded and they kept coming, closer and closer.

CHAPTER 12

Out of the forest, into the clearing, rode Washakie and Toosnamp. They were leading a third horse. The huge body of the elk was tied to it.

"Hey! I'm over here," Nick yelled and waved at Washakie. Then he remembered. He clamped his hands over his mouth and looked toward the Indians at his left. There was nothing there.

Washakie and Toosnamp rode toward Nick. "Why are you here, Brother? You were left to guard the elk. Some wild animal might have eaten it."

"I saw some strange Indians sneaking around," Nick said. "I followed them to see what they were doing. I think they were after our horses."

Nick led the way to the place where the three men had lain. He was glad he didn't have to tell Washakie that he had run away from the elk and lost it altogether. He had made fun of the Indian boys for being afraid of a bear. He wasn't going to let anyone know that he was afraid of an elk.

"They are gone, Brother. You have let them get away," Washakie said. He sounded gruff, but he had a twinkle in his eyes.

Nick knew that Washakie was teasing him. "I didn't need to follow them," he said. "They didn't take any of *my* horses."

"You are wise, Brother." Washakie grinned.

"If those men had been friends, they would not have hidden themselves in the forest," Toosnamp said, thoughtfully.

Washakie nodded agreement. "I will send the scouts to track them. We do not want to make trouble with another tribe, but we cannot let anybody steal our horses."

Washakie presented the dead elk with the perfect hide to Hanabi that evening. She was at Old Mother's tepee. It seemed as if she was always there.

"This will make you a white dress that has no holes in it," Washakie told her.

"Why did you not cut the throat?" Old Mother asked him. "The meat will not keep with the blood set in it."

"Little Brother was waiting for it to die when he saw some Crows. He tracked them to save our horses. He will soon be a warrior," Washakie bragged to the women.

"He will be a brave chief of the Shoshones," Old Mother proudly told Hanabi. "If we roast the meat today, it will be all right."

The rest of the day, Nick strutted about. He liked to be called Tae-cum-a-dai. That meant The Boy Who Saved the Horses. That sounded a lot better to him than Yagaiki, The Crier.

"The Crows are attacking!" They had been asleep for hours when that call rang through the camp. Nick leaped from his bed of skins. Washakie gathered up his weapons and turned to leave the tent. Nick grabbed his own bow and slung his pouch of arrows across his shoulder. As he started to duck out the door, Old Mother grabbed his shirt.

"Where do you think you are going?" she demanded.

"You and Washakie both said that I was a warrior, and warriors protect the tribe from the enemy. I am going to fight the enemy with Washakie."

"Not tonight you aren't," said Old Mother. "Tonight you are going with me to hide from the Crows in the rushes. The men will fight the enemy. Washakie, make him come with me. He cannot go out and fight the Crows."

Washakie laughed. "Brother is only fooling," he said, pushing Nick toward Old Mother. "He doesn't want to fight the Crows. They didn't take any of his horses. I am going to guard the camp tonight. Brother is going with you."

Old Mother hung on tightly to Nick's shirt anyway, and towed him along with her toward the stream.

"What's going on?" Nick demanded. He stumbled over somebody's leg in the dark.

"Owee! Watch where you walk. You stepped on me." Nick

recognized Boni's voice. He felt a little better. He wasn't the only big boy crouching in the weeds with his mother.

"Has anyone seen my little girl?" A woman's voice came close. She wailed loudly as she felt her way along through the cattails.

"I'm hiding over here," a child's voice called.

"Come with me," the woman said, sniffing loudly.

"I want to stay with my friends," the child objected.

"Oh no!" the woman wailed. "You must be with me. How else can I know if the Crows scalp you?"

At that, a squawk of voices, both children's and women's filled the air. *They make so much noise that we'll never be able to hear the Crows if they do come,* Nick thought.

"Owee-Owee-owee." "Aiii-aiii-aiii."

"Are the Crows here, yet?"

"I don't like it here! I'm cold!"

"This is stupid," Nick said to Old Mother. "Why do we hide like rabbits and then howl like coyotes? The whole world knows where we are hiding."

"The enemy would never come out here in the darkness to catch us. But we want to be ready if the do," Old Mother told him.

"This is really so stupid," Nick said again. "Are the Crows as much cowards as our Indians?"

"Yes," said Old Mother. "People everywhere are much alike."

Nick remembered back to Grantsville. All the people for miles around had run to the safety of the walls of the settlement so that the Indians couldn't get them. He had been little then, and he had bawled as loudly as anybody. The men had waited on the walls with their guns ready. The women and children had hidden in the meeting room. Nick had always felt cheated when no Indians ever came to fight. I guess this isn't much different, he thought. He laid his head in Old Mother's lap and looked up at the zillions of stars. The night didn't seem so dark now. He guessed it was all right for every body to bawl. It sort of made things more exciting.

When Buffalo Slayer, the father of the twins, came to tell them that no Crows were coming, everyone went quietly to his own tepee. They were stiff and cold and glad to get back to bed.

*

The next day they moved again. The days grew hot as they drifted south, along the edge of the mountains. Fish were plentiful, though small. Elk and deer were everywhere. Hanabi had plenty of animal brains to cure her elk skin, to make it as white as snow. The smoked meat was pounded to a pulp in readiness for making pemmican.

The currants on the hill are ripe," Old Mother said casually one evening. "Tomorrow we will gather them. They must be dried to add to our pemmican,"

"Can I go?" Nick asked.

"This is a chore that all the women and children must do. We must pick fast before the birds and the bears eat them all."

It was a noisy crowd of women and children who rode their ponies to the hillside next morning. The packhorses carried baskets for holding berries, but the boys carried their bows and arrows, and their lassos.

Might as well be prepared, thought Nick.

The young grouse and pine hens were just right for eating. The women were experienced in berry picking. They carefully gathered the ripe, fragrant clumps of fruit that gleamed like red jewels on a string.

"Leave the berries on their stems," Old Mother told Nick. She lined a basket with large fern leaves and poured her small bowl of berries into it. "The stems protect the berries from smashing."

Nick put as many berries into his mouth as he did in the basket. The tart sweet fruit puckered his lips, then trickled down his throat like honey. His red-stained fingers clung stickily together. He licked the sweet juice from them. Nobody nagged him to put the berries in the basket.

"Come on, Brother. Let's go rope that stump at the bottom of the hill," Boni called to Nick.

Nick left Old Mother and followed Boni. Ahead of them, Mopi and Yagamont raced each other, sliding and stumbling down the steep trail. They had done girl's work long enough. Now it was time to get about the business of being braves. Their horses were tethered beside a sparkling stream that trickled from beneath a rock and splashed down the tiny waterway that reached down the slope. Mopi, who ran fastest, made a flying leap and landed on his pony's back.

"Boni, you can untie my horse now," Mopi said. I want to have the first turn to lasso the stump."

Boni panted breathlessly to a stop beside Mopi. "If you are going to ride like the wind, be sure that you are not tied to the ground," he said. But he good-naturedly loosed Mopi's horse and then his own. He dropped into line behind Mopi.

Nick ran down the hill after Boni and jumped over Yagamont, who lay laughing in the path. A root had tripped him and he had sprawled headlong and rolled to the bottom of the hill.

"Here I come! Get out of my way!" Nick called to the others. He quickly mounted his pinto and swung his lasso about his head.

"Help me! Help me!" A shriek of pain and fear echoed down the mountain. "A bear has killed my girl! My girl is dead!"

A screaming woman dashed down the hillside toward them. People popped out of the berry bushes all up and down the hillside. Mothers yanked their little ones along by the arms, and yelled at the larger ones to come quickly. Nick slapped his pinto on the flank with his rope, urging it up the hill. He nearly ran over the women and children who poured down the trail toward him, screaming and crying.

"Come on, fellows," hollered Nick. "I think I can see the bear going up ahead of me!"

A great silver-grey bear lumbered along up the hill. It could not move fast. The girl it held by the shoulder, dragged along, catching on the bushes, holding back the bear.

Nick charged the bear, lashing it furiously across the rump with his lasso. The bear dropped the girl and turned with a roar to face its tormentor.

The giant shaggy beast rose to its hind legs, its cruel fangs bared. Bellowing menacingly, it came at Nick, swaying from side to side as it came. Nick lashed out with his rope again and again, across the animal's nose, across its eyes and ears. Over and over he struck, driven by fear. He couldn't stop. Again and again Nick swung at the bear while his pinto mare quivered beneath his knees.

The bear dropped to all four feet. It backed up two steps, then turned tail and fled, whimpering as it ran.

Nick slid from his horse. His legs had turned to water. They refused to hold him up, and he fell to the ground.

"Stop that!" he told himself. "You don't have time for this nonsense! That old bear could come back at any second."

Nick crawled to where the girl lay face down. There was no blood on her but she looked dead. Nick rolled her onto her back.

"Oh God!" he exclaimed. It's Raida!" He stood up and cupped his hands to his mouth. "Hey, you boys! Help me! I need help!" There was no answer.

Quickly he looked around him. There was no one there. Odd. Everyone was gone.

Raida's eyelids fluttered. "Owee—I am hurt," she whispered.

"Are you all right?" Nick asked.

"Could I have a drink of water?" Raida answered.

Nick found a little bowl beside the trail. *Someone's berry-picking bowl,* he thought. He filled it swiftly with water from the little trickle at their side. He lifted Raida's head while she swallowed a small amount.

"That bear bit me on my neck and it made me go to sleep," said Raida. "I feel better now."

"We had better get out of here before it comes back," said Nick. "Can you stand up? You are too heavy for me to carry."

"I will try," she said.

With Nick's help, Raida succeeded in climbing on to the pinto. She held tightly to the saddle and Nick led his horse down the hill.

When they were about halfway back to the camp, Raida said, "I am better now. You can get up here on the horse with me. We can ride faster."

That is what Nick did. The sound reached them as they approached. Wails and cries hung over the whole camp like a cloud. Now Nick knew where all the people had gone.

"What is wrong? Have the Crows come?" Raida asked Nick.

"I don't think so," he said. I think they are bawling because the bear ate you."

"I am right here. The bear didn't eat me," she said.

"It would have. They didn't even try to save you. They are nothing but a bunch of cowards." Nick muttered, more to himself than to her.

After Nick had delivered Raida to her mother, he went slowly to his own tepee. Old Mother saw him coming and tried to hug him.

"I thought the bear had eaten you too," she said.

Nick shook her off. He didn't want any part of that right now. He was furious at her. He was furious with the whole bribe of them. How could three hundred people leave one girl to be eaten by a bear?

"Where have you been?" Old Mother demanded. "I was worried when you weren't with Boni and Yagamont and the twin boy. What have you been doing?"

"Not much," Nick said. He turned and stomped away in disgust.

*

The dark had settled over the camp when Mopi appeared silently at Washakie's tent.

"My father wants Brother to come," Mopi said to Washakie.

"Go to Buffalo Slayer," Washakie told Nick.

"Come with me, Washakie," Nick said. He wasn't sure of what

101

to expect.

At the tepee of Buffalo Slayer, Raida lay on a bed of skins; her mother was seated beside her, massaging her shoulder.

"My girl said you took her from the mouth of the bear. If you hadn't done so, the bear would surely have eaten her. You are a brave boy. That bear might have eaten you too. The bears have a hatred of Real People. They want to slay all of us, especially the giant grizzlies. When you are old enough, you may have my girl to be your squaw." Buffalo Slayer told Nick.

"No thanks," said Nick. "Raida is the best girl I know. I am glad the bear didn't eat her. But I think I will live with Old Mother when I grow up, like Washakie does."

"Why didn't anyone come to help me drive the bear away?" Nick asked Washakie, as they walked through the dark, back to their own lodge.

"The women and children could not drive the bear away. They could only run. Bears are very dangerous. It was only by chance that the bear did not kill you. They must eat a lot in a hurry so they will be fat enough to sleep all winter. If they believe they are losing their food, they will kill anything in sight. They have been known to kill three or four people at a time. And if you are dead, you are good for nothing but bear food." Washakie put his hand on Nick's shoulder.

"It seems to me that the Indians are cowards. I still think that when someone needs help, you should help and not run for you life," Nick argued.

"That may be so," said Washakie, "but quite often, your life is the only thing of value you have."

CHAPTER 13

All summer, Crows raided the horse pasture in the night. It didn't matter where the Shoshones camped, the Crows came after dark to steal more horses. The scouts tried to follow them, but they always came back from the chase, empty-handed.

"Aren't you going after the horses? Are going to let those thieving Crows get away with them?" Nick asked Washakie.

The Crows had once more, stolen into camp and driven away ten horses.

"That is a decision for the War Chief," Washakie said. "The hunting party is going to hunt for buffalo."

I think Washakie is an old woman, thought Nick. Washakie worries more of women's things than he does of stolen horses, especially since he brought Hanabi to live with us in our tepee.

Three days later a group of young warriors drove twenty-three Crow horses into camp. *It is a good thing that not all the men in the tribe are old women,* Nick thought.

"The Crows are camped on the other side of the buttes. We saw then when we were trying to go to the buffalo hunting ground. When we found them, we brought some of their horses to replete what they have stolen from us," one of the warriors told Washakie.

"They are going to make war on someone. It will probably be us," a second man told those who watched.

Washakie was gone when Nick awoke the next morning. The War Chief called all the men together.

"The unbroken horses must be sent away," he said. We will take them to the Paiupa River. The band of the father of Buffalo Slayer's wife will care for them for us. Then the Crows will not steal them."

Oh sure, thought Nick. These cowards not only run away from bears, they run away from a bunch of people named after birds. I bet the Crows would not run from us.

That afternoon the boys and young men separated the mustangs from the broken horses. Next morning, twenty seasoned warriors drove the wild horses from the camp and headed them toward the south. The women and children dismantled the camp. Soon possessions were stacked about in great piles. The remaining horses were corralled nearby.

That was when the strangers began arriving. About a hundred warriors rode in from the west, over the mountain range. Several hundred came from the south. Nick was amazed. No one had said a word, yet fighting men came from all directions.

Early in the morning, three days after the horses had been driven south, the fighting men gathered together for a pow-wow.

"The Crows believe we are afraid of them. We must fight them now or go back along the trail we came on," the War Chief said to the council of men who sat around the fire discussing their strategy.

"That is the way I see it," said Washakie. Nick looked around, startled. He hadn't even known Washakie had come back.

"The Crows are camped where we must cross the river. They want to keep us from our buffalo grounds. I saw many Crow fighting men, there. The warriors from the entire Crow Nation are waiting for us. Now is the time to show them that we will fight for our rights." Washakie looked solemnly about.

"Yes!"

"That is so!"

"We will fight to the death! We cannot turn back now," the War Chief said again.

That night, everyone rolled into his robe and slept under the stars. There were so many people lying all around that Nick couldn't turn over without rolling on someone. A tight knot filled his stomach. Maybe he had misjudged Washakie. Maybe the Shoshones weren't cowards.

Horses, blowing and stomping, woke Nick early. The warriors were mounted and ready to ride. They looked mighty fierce. Black paint, mingled with red, yellow and blue, made grotesque masks of their faces.

If they can't kill the enemy with their spears or arrows, maybe they will scare them to death, thought Nick.

Each man had a white feather in his hair and a broad band of cloth over the right shoulder and under the left arm.

"There must be a thousand Crows on the other side of the hill," one of the mounted men said.

"We will go to our hunting ground if we must kill ten thousand Crows," another answered.

That didn't sound like much of a joke to Nick, but all of the warriors laughed loudly.

With the War Chief in the lead, the warriors rode slowly away in single file. Washakie gave last minute instructions to the old men who were left behind to guard the camp. He then galloped his horse to join the slow moving column of riders. There he took his position at the rear of the line. The war party rounded the knoll and was lost from sight.

The women went about the daily chores as if it was a normal day. They fetched wood and water. They fed the children. They rolled and stored the sleeping robes.

Old Morgoni, who had charge of the camp, now urged the boys to saddle all the riding horses. The knot in Nick's stomach eased. *There isn't going really going to be any war,* he thought. Then away in the distance, faint popping sounds began.

"They are fighting now," Morgoni told the waiting camp. "That is the War Chief's gun you can hear. Some of the Crows must have firesticks also. It is time for us to go to the stream that we crossed, about a mile back along the trail. We will make our camp there. We will be staying for awhile."

They quickly moved all their belongings back to the new camp. Old Mother, Hanabi, and Nick were putting the finishing fastenings on their tepee when Raida rushed up to them.

"Look!" She pointed to the hill, behind which the fighting men had disappeared.

Men on horseback swarmed across the top of the hill. Whoops and yells carried to them across the distance. Warriors with tomahawks hacked at other warriors, pushing them from the top of the hill and down the slope toward the camp.

At the top of the hill, arrows flew through the air. Now and then, the pop of a gunshot was heard. The men and horses were getting closer and closer. The whole top of the hill was covered with fighting men. There must be at least fifteen-hundred warriors on the hill and spilling over into the plains below.

"We are winning! We are winning!" cried Yagamont.

"Oh no," said Mopi quietly. "We are losing. See the white shoulder bands. Our warriors are being driven back."

Old Mother dashed to her pile of belongings and pawed through it. "I'll get my knife and cut their hearts out if they come here!" she shrieked.

Nick looked around. Other women all over camp were also hunting in their packs for weapons. They were ready to fight the Crows, too, if they needed to.

"It would be wiser if you finished making camp," Old Morgoni said. "Men are being wounded. They will soon need care and a place to lie down."

The women reluctantly went to complete their tasks. The old men rode in a circle about the camp. The horses were as nervous as the women. It was all the old men could do to keep the herd from stampeding. While the camp rose around them, the children watched the fighting men on the hillside.

"There is Washakie!" shouted Nick. "See his buckskin horse!"

Washakie galloped from one pocket of fighting to another. He would stop for only a few seconds, then gallop to another place. The warriors seemed to rally wherever he stopped.

"He is giving them orders," Raida said to Hanabi. "He knows how to win."

It seemed the girl was right. The men with the white bands on their chests began to push the others back up the hill. Riderless horses ran aimlessly among the fighting.

"Come on, Mopi!" yelled Nick. "See those horses—a lot of men must be hurt. They need us to help get the best of those rotten Crows!"

He didn't wait for an answer, but bolted toward his pinto.

"Stop that boy!" Old Mother barked.

Instantly, old Morogoni deftly dropped his lasso over Nick's shoulders.

"You must wait a while, Little Brother," Morogoni said to him. The old man climbed stiffly from his horse and took the rope from Nick's body. "You will be a great warrior some day, but do not be in such a hurry."

"I might have killed a whole flock of Crows if you had let me alone," said Nick, pouting.

"Someday you will have your time," Morogoni said.

As they watched, the fighting warriors disappeared back over the crest of the hill.

"We are winning now!" shouted Yagamont. This time no one argued.

The sounds of the fighting grew further and further away. Soon they had nothing left to do but wait. The sun dropped past the middle of the sky, going away from the fighting. Still the women and children waited.

Maybe the warriors went over into the Crow country and ran into an ambush. Maybe the men were all dead. Nick tried not to think such gloomy thoughts, but the men had been gone such a long time.

Sometime after the sun was gone to bed, the warriors returned. Eight hundred had ridden away in a slow and stately column. Now, fewer than half that number came back, galloping bent for Hell.

Everyone talked at once. The Crows were running away. Washakie and the other warriors were trying to get around them to cut them off from their tribe. They had come to get fresh horses. In the morning, the Shoshones would attack again. They needed a hundred horses so that they could chase the Crows. Many brave men were wounded. Twenty-five were dead.

When they heard that, half of the women and children of the camp sent up a wail.

"This is stupid," said Nick to Old Mother and Hanabi. "They don't even know who is dead and here they are bawling their heads off. You could hear them for miles."

"You hush," said Hanabi. "Tomorrow it could be our turn to cry."

Old Mother looked startled. "They can take two of my horses to chase the Crows," she said.

"I guess they can have my grey horse," said Nick glumly. Hanabi had made him ashamed of himself.

More riders kept coming into camp all night. The wounded who could ride helped the warriors who couldn't help themselves. The War Chief himself had an arrow in his leg and another in his arm, yet he escorted a man with a missing eye and no nose. It was nearly morning before the sounds of horses arriving were no longer heard. The last thing Nick heard as he drifted off to sleep was a man groaning as he was helped to a bed of skins nearby.

When he awoke, Nick looked across the tepee to Washakie's bed. The man in it groaned as he tried to move. It wasn't Washakie. Nick could tell that. When he got up and looked at the man's face, he recognized Toosnamp.

"What happened to you?" asked Nick.

"I was shot in the leg with an arrow first, but I did not fall. Then I was shot in the arm and once more in the leg. When my horse was killed, a Crow stuck a spear in my side. If my horse hadn't fallen I would have killed that Crow. But I missed his heart and shot him in the shoulder. He fought very hard."

Old Mother came into the tepee with the medicine man.

"The War Chief and the warriors who could ride have gone to help Washakie chase the Crows," she told Toosnamp. The medicine man will take care of you now."

She beckoned for Nick follow her from the tepee.

Nick started to leave Toosnamp alone in the tepee with the old medicine man. He didn't know why he did it, but suddenly he pointed at the old man and blurted out, "Watch out for that old devil. He might finish what the Crows started."

Old Mother grabbed Nick by the arm and yanked him from the tent.

"If you don't learn to quiet your tongue you may have to eat your words," she scolded.

CHAPTER 14

Old Mother kept Nick at her side as she went from tepee to tepee, visiting the wounded. There was a wounded man, a husband, a son, or a brother in almost half of the lodges. Nick counted one hundred eighteen. Some of them didn't look to him as if they would live through the day. The weather was hot, and the flies had come from miles around to torment the poor wounded.

"Get some sagebrush and build a smoky fire inside the tepee next to the wounded," Old Mother said. "That will drive out the flies. Be sure to leave an opening for the fresh air to come in, so the men can breathe. Run, girls, gather a big pile of sage. The limbs will make smoke and the leaves will make tea to bathe the wounds."

Sixteen men died in camp that day. When the warriors came back that evening, they were subdued. The Crows had eluded them in the forest, but they had won a great victory. They could now go to the buffalo grounds.

The dead from the camp were carried back to the battleground. There, all the dead Shoshone warriors, forty-one in all, were tossed into a deep crevasse, along with all the slain horses—their own and the ones of the Crows. The bodies of the thieving Crows that littered the field were promptly scalped, then left there for the wolves to eat.

Nick wanted to scream, "Stop it! Stop it!" but the bile rose in his throat and choked off the words. He couldn't watch those women with the long knives going from body to body, stripping off the hair to give to the wounded warriors.

"Why didn't you cut the scalps off the dead Shoshones and send them to the Crows?" he said. He couldn't keep the disgust from his voice.

"You hush," said Old Mother. She held up the hair of the dead Crow that she had just finished removing. "You don't know what you are saying. The Crows would have killed all of us if they could have. The Shoshones have a right to the Crow trophies of war."

"In that case I'll get a few trophies for myself," said Nick. He turned his back on the Indian woman and grabbed up the arrows that lay thick nearby.

"Throw them down at once!" Old Mother demanded. "The old men will gather everything here that belonged to the Crows."

"What do they want with them?" Nick threw the arrows as far as he could.

"They will be saved for use, later. The arrows will give our warriors good medicine the next time they fight a war."

This is so stupid, thought Nick again, blinking back tears. The war is hardly over and already these idiots are planning the next one.

"I'm going to camp," he told Old Mother. "There is nothing here for me."

When the rest of the tribe arrived back at the camp, the trophies were dumped in a pile in the middle of the camp. Nick had never seen so much stuff in one pile: buffalo robes, trade blankets, saddle blankets, war bonnets, bead belts, animal teeth necklaces, medicine pouches, anything an Indian warrior might carry to war. The ponies that wandered among the slain warriors had been rounded up also. This loot was divided among the fighting men. The War Chief and Washakie got double portions. Mopi stood in for his father. Buffalo Slayer had died on the field of battle. The families of the other slain men also received a share of the spoils.

Well, at least they are fair, thought Nick.

The mourning of the dead lasted five days. The camp howled and bawled for the whole time. Nick was glad that the dead had all been put in one big grave. He didn't have to touch every one, that way, and say he was sorry they were gone. He *was* sorry, though.

"May the Great Spirit welcome you. May your courage go before you," said Washakie. He had been the spokesman for the whole tribe. That is when they began throwing in the rocks.

The camp rested two weeks so that the wounded had time to heal. When finally they did get to the buffalo country, the hunt was much slower than it had been the year before. Without Buffalo

Slayer to sneak up to the buffalo heels and cut their tendons, the killings dragged on.

"I will practice. On the next hunt I will be ready to take my father's place. Then my name will no longer be Mopi—Came Last. Then I will be Son of Buffalo Slayer," said Mopi, importantly.

Mopi was different. Nick couldn't tell exactly how. He was still a braggart. He was still a bully. But something had changed. Maybe it was because his mother no longer made him help Raida with the women's work.

"I am going to take my buffalo robes and my extra horses to the rendezvous," Mopi bragged to his friends.

Nobody said "Hooo! You are only a boy." Everyone knew that because he was the oldest male in his wigwam, and because his father had died in battle, they were now *his* horses and buffalo robes.

A heavy feeling surrounded the camp. The injured men still sat huddled before the tepees. The wound in Toosnamp's side continually drained a bloody fluid. Finally, the toothless, smelly old medicine man opened the wound and cut off two of Toosnamp's ribs.

"Now the hole will heal up," he said.

Nick thought that Toosnamp looked sicker than ever. That's the way with Indian medicine, he thought. They have to kill you to cure you.

All the while the women worked steadily. There were hides to tan and meat to cure. A smoky fire was kept going all day and all night, to tan the buffalo hides just right.

The young braves allowed Mopi and his friends to join them when they went out to hunt deer or elk. It was time for them to prepare to be the warriors to replace the injured and slain.

Once when they were returning from a hunt, a young bear had the misfortune to wander too close to camp. Nick kicked his pinto pony in the ribs, swinging his lasso wide about his head.

"Are you cowards going to let this puny bear get away from you

113

this time?" he whooped. His lasso flew out from him and caught the bear by the front paw.

Flying Eagle, one of the braves, joined Nick in the chase. He dropped his lasso around the bear's neck.

"Quick! You go one way around that tree and I'll go the other," he yelled to Nick.

They soon had the bear tied securely to the tall pine that stood alone in the clearing. All the rest of the boys now entered into the excitement. They rode their ponies in a circle about the tree, shooting the bear repeatedly until it resembled a porcupine with arrows sticking out all over it.

"Let's give it to Raida," said Nick when it was dead. The others agreed, so they gave the dead bear to Raida.

"Come over and eat with us tonight," said Raida's Mother. "Raida wants you all to help her eat the bear." The woman laughed uproariously. All the boys laughed too. Nick thought it was a good joke, but Raida didn't even smile.

The bear hide was the first skin that Raida had tanned all by herself. She had left the hair on so it could be used for a rug.

"It has many holes in it," said Boni, when she held it up for her friends to see. "It will make nothing but a sleeping robe."

"It is so rough to touch," Yagamont said. "It would itch you if you tried to sleep in it."

"I think it is nice," said Nick. "You did a good job. It isn't your fault if it has holes in it. These boys are the ones who made the holes."

*

When the hides were all prepared and the work was all finished, most of the camp got ready to go to Great Salt Lake City. It was time again to rendezvous with the traders.

"Get some coffee and trade blankets for me. When I was at the rendezvous last time, I saw a big bundle of soft red cloth. I think they called it 'flannel'. I would like to have some of that. I could use it inside the moccasins to keep my feet warm when the snows come," said Old Mother.

Washakie and Hanabi were to take thirty-eight Crow horses to trade.

"What are you going to trade them for?" Nick asked Washakie.

"I will trade for whatever I can get. I hope I can get a firestick and some powder and lead. Many white men do not want to trade guns to the Indians, but thirty-eight horses are a lot of horses. Do you want us to bring anything for you, Brother?"

"If you take me, I will trade your horses for five guns," said Nick.

"Not this time, Brother," said Washakie. "Mother needs you to help her care for our horses and the wounded men. They must be moved to the Bear Lake where we will meet you when we return."

Nick knew why Washakie wouldn't let him go with them to the rendezvous. It was close to where Pa and Ma lived, and Old Mother was afraid that he might go home. If she asked him, he would tell her not to worry. She didn't need to worry at all. He didn't want to go back to Grantsville. He was already home. He might get upset with some of their ways but here among the Indians, he wasn't always wrong.

Nick watched Washakie, Hanabi, and the rest of the travelers ride away. Almost everyone in camp had taken their trade items and left for the Great Salt Lake City. He felt that they were angry with him. He wasn't used to being left behind.

Feeling sad, Nick had gone out to hunt birds. He had killed one sage hen with his bow and arrow. Now he sauntered toward home. One bird wasn't enough to feed Toosnamp and Old Mother and himself, but they could at least get a taste of it. If that ugly yellow mutt hadn't come along to chase them away, he would have shot the whole flock of sage chickens for supper. Nick knew most of the dogs in the camp, but that yellow one was a stranger. It must belong to one of the people who had come to travel with Washakie to the rendezvous. Well the dog was gone now.

"What in the world?" Something had hit the back of his leg just below the knee. *Oh boy, it hurts!* Nick dropped the sage hen and grabbed the back of his leg. Blood trickled between his fingers. That sneaky little mongrel had helped himself to a chunk of Nick's leg.

"You get away from me, you lousy flea bag!" Nick yelled at the dog.

But the beast crouched beside the trail with lips drawn back and sharp yellow teeth bared. Its eyes glinted with meanness and a growl rumbled in its throat. It slunk to the sage hen on the ground where Nick had dropped it. It seemed to declare ownership of the bird, daring Nick to do anything about it.

"I did not run from a bear. I am sure not going to run from you," Nick told the dog. He aimed his arrow at the dog. He was so close that he could not miss. He sent the arrow flying at the dog. It hit with a thud. The arrowhead went right through the dog's belly and came out the other side.

"Kiii-yiii kiii-yiii!" The dog yelped and howled, then ran straight to one of the tepees.

"Give me back my arrow!" Nick chased right behind the dog.

A woman and a big girl stepped out of the tepee to see what all the ruckus was about.

"Oh, poor puppy," the girl said. She knelt to comfort the injured dog. The dog, however, had no desire to be comforted. He snarled at the girl and dashed away, carrying Nick's arrow with it, the head sticking out one side and the feathers out the other.

"It's that white boy, the one who tried to knock your brains out," the woman screamed.

She threw her arms around Nick and shoved him to the ground.

"Tie his feet, Patooli. This time we will get his scalp! This time we will cut his heart out! This time Washakie is not here to save him!"

While the woman sat on top of Nick, the girl, Patooli fetched a leather thong and tried to tie Nick's feet together.

Nick wasn't finished yet. He kicked and squirmed, bucking the woman to the ground. He then leaped to his feet and ran.

Patooli and her mother raced close behind.

Nick's leg pained him fiercely, but he was not going to let those female savages get hold of him again. He glanced over his shoulder. They were gaining on him. Nick was sure they meant to scalp him this time. He had to get away. Instead he ran into someone who put his arms around Nick and held him fast.

"Why are you running so fast, Little Brother?" asked Toosnamp.

Nick sagged against him in relief. Toosnamp hobbled around for a little exercise, and Nick was grateful.

"What do you want with the boy?" Toosnamp asked Patooli's mother. "What has he done to you?"

"That white devil is evil! Once he tried to kill my girl. Now, he has killed my girl's dog. He makes trouble wherever he goes."

"Did you do this?" Toosnamp asked Nick.

"Their mangy dog bit me for no reason, and I shot him. He isn't dead yet, but he will be." Nick showed Toosnamp the angry flesh that hung from the calf of his leg.

"This is bad," said Toosnamp. He touched the bite. "Go to your tepee. I will bring the medicine man."

As he headed for home, Nick heard Toosnamp scoulding the woman. "You have a big problem. I think *you* are the troublemaker. You just got back to this camp, and already you are in trouble. This time Washakie will banish you from the Real People forever."

"We did not hurt him," the woman protested.

At the tepee, Old Mother looked at Nick's leg and began to cry loudly. "Oh, you have been crippled. The medicine man will want to cut off the leg. Oh my poor boy."

"Nobody will cut off my leg. Just leave it alone and it will be all right," said Nick.

When the medicine man saw the wound, he clucked his tongue.

117

He sprinkled the bite with a white powder from a dried buffalo horn and bound it up with big bitter dock leaves.

"Where is the animal who did this thing?" he asked.

"He is out there somewhere, running around with my arrow in him," said Nick. "He will die soon."

"He must be killed before he dies," declared the smelly old man. "I must kill him." He whirled around twice and ducked out.

"I don't want that crazy old man to touch me, again," said Nick.

Old Mother looked as if she was going to cry again.

"I'll be all right," Nick assured her. "Just leave me alone."

He turned his face to the tepee wall and curled up into a ball, holding his throbbing leg.

Soon Nick knew that he wasn't going to be all right. His leg burned with fierce pain, and had turned an angry red. It was so swollen he could not bend his knee. When the medicine man returned, Nick let him bind his blob of powder and leaves to the bite again.

"The dog is dead," the medicine man told Old Mother. "Now the boy may recover."

The throbbing pain did not go away. It got worse. The leg swelled more each day, but the camp had to move. The grass for the horses was gone. Old Mother and the other aged people had the nearly impossible task of packing the whole place by themselves.

Nick couldn't lie around and watch the old woman struggling to catch all the horses. He fashioned himself a pair of crutches from two forked sticks. Hopping around with the aid of his sticks, he helped where he could.

"How do you do that?" asked Toosnamp. "Could you make me some sticks to walk on?"

"You bet," said Nick.

Injured men from all over camp were soon walking on forked stick crutches. They set to work to pack the camp for moving and as they worked, moving around, they seemed to grow stronger.

But Nick's leg, despite the green weed poultice, grew worse. When the camp was set up at the next site, Nick was so sick that he climbed onto his bed and resignedly lay there. He didn't want to die, but he felt so bad he thought he might. The leg was swollen to twice its size. A red line climbed from the bite below the knee, to the middle of Nick's thigh. His head pounded every time his heart beat.

When the medicine man came, he rubbed his hands together.

"It is as I feared," he said to Old Mother. "I must cut off the leg."

"No you don't!" screamed Nick. "You get your poison weeds off me and you get out of here. I would rather die than let you cut off my leg! Get him out of here, Mother! Get him out of here!"

Nick was exhausted from his outburst. He dropped back on his buffalo robe and sobbed in despair.

"You go," Old Mother said to the wild-looking man with his stinking feathers and bones. "You will not cut off my boy's leg today."

Quickly she pushed him from her tent. Two days later the camp moved again, and left Old Mother and Nick in their tepee beside a stream.

"Brother, last night I had a dream that Washakie came and killed a sage-chicken. I put the warm entrails on your leg and they pulled all the poison out of your leg. Then your leg got better," the old woman told Nick.

"I don't want any more of your Indian medicine," Nick told her weakly. "Indian ways aren't for white people."

"But you are my son," Old Mother said. She began to cry. "You are a Shoshone now."

Nick turned his back on her and refused to eat. He knew now that he was really going to die. His head hurt, his leg had gone black. He was hot all over and he didn't want to see her cry anymore.

CHAPTER 15

As Nick feverishly tossed and turned, rolled and tumbled on his bed of buffalo skins, he lost all track of time. Once he opened his eyes to see the old woman sitting beside him with her blanket covering her head. She didn't even look at him. He allowed himself to float back to oblivion. Deep in his fevered brain, he thought he heard someone talking.

When next he opened his eyes, the pain was gone. Washakie was there beside him.

"Where did you come from?" Nick asked Washakie. "I didn't know you had died too."

"You're not dead, Little Brother," Washakie assured Nick. "You have been very sick. When the caravan arrived at the meeting place at Bear Lake last week, Toosnamp told me about your leg. I came quickly when I heard. Mother told me of her dream. I killed a sage hen for her. When she put the entrails on your wound, you began to get better. The Great Spirit gave her that message. Today you are awake. That medicine man had a hatred for you. He had been putting poison weeds on your leg. If you had not been so strong, you might really have died. But now that you are awake, we must join the tribe."

Old Mother entered the tepee, and took her place beside Nick's bed. Nick reached out and pulled her to him. He kissed her softly on her cheek. "I guess I am a Shoshone. I am glad that you used your Indian medicine on me." Then he dropped off to sleep.

The next day, even though Nick's leg was still too sore to straddle a horse, Washakie strung a buffalo robe hammock between two horses. Here, Nick rode with a minimum of jolting.

Washakie watched Nick with concern. "Am I going too fast for you, Brother?" he asked again and again.

"I am fine," Nick replied.

"Are you certain you don't want me to slow down?" Washakie again questioned Nick.

"No, I am fine," Nick assured again. "You can run the horses if you want to."

Washakie laughed. "It is plain that you are recovering," he said. "I think we have time to walk."

*

Nick healed rapidly. Within a month, he was well enough to think about breaking more horses. So many of the working horses had been traded at the rendezvous that the tribe was short of packhorses and riding horses. A group of the young braves had ridden to the Paiupa river and returned with the unbroken horses.

Nick and Yagamont were busy in the horse pasture when they saw Pocatello and his warriors arrive. The hair along Nick's neck prickled, and a knot tightened in his stomach. *I am still afraid of that man,* he thought.

"I'm tired," Nick told Yagamont. "Let's go back to camp."

"Pocatello makes me tired, too," Yagamont agreed. "He only comes when he has been making trouble for someone."

Pocatello and his warriors were there for some secret purpose. Even though the weather was still very warm, the council met inside Washakie's large elk-skin tepee. The children and women were not allowed to go in at all.

"What terrible things are they keeping from us?" Old Mother asked Hanabi and Nick. They were sitting at some distance from their tent. "I know they are plotting to some awful thing. That evil man, Pocatello, wants us to do some bad thing."

"Maybe that is not so," said Hanabi. "Last time he was here he came to trade."

"But why should they keep us out of our own lodge if they were only trading?" Old Mother dropped her head to her hands. "I have a great fear in me."

The meeting dragged on. For two evenings, when the men of the tribe left the tepee, their faces were drawn and grim. The morning of the third day, the War Chief came to the entrance of the tepee and

122

beckoned Nick to come inside.

"I knew! I knew!" wailed Old Mother. "I knew that that dog, Pocatello, was making trouble for us—and in my very own tepee!"

She shoved her way into the tent. "If you are talking about my boys, I am going to be here."

Washakie looked at the War Chief. Pocatello scowled.

"Let her stay," said the War Chief.

Old Mother stood beside Nick and clung tightly to him.

"How long have you lived in our camp?" the War Chief asked Nick.

"I came at the last rendezvous. It is one year," answered Nick.

"How old were you when you came?" Morogoni was the next to ask a question.

"I was twelve," Nick said.

"Why did you come?" Toosnamp smiled at Nick as he spoke.

"You know," answered Nick.

"Tell the council," Toosnamp said.

"I wasn't happy at Grantsville, and I wanted the pinto pony," Nick told them.

"Washakie paid to have you stolen." Pocatello was emphatic about his statement. "He had you stolen because his mother wanted a white boy."

Old Mother tightened her grip on Nick's arm.

"I don't know about that," said Nick. "Toosnamp gave me the pony and I came because I wanted it."

"I told Toosnamp to offer the boy the pony. It had belonged to Buffalo Slayer, who has gone on ahead to the Great Spirit. I gave Buffalo Slayer two horses and Morogoni gave him one to replace the pinto. We wanted Mother to be happy. Toosnamp was only to bring the boy from his white home if he wanted to come. He was not to steal him away," Washakie told the council.

"No one made me come. I ran off from my home myself," said Nick.

"Have you been happy with the Shoshones?" the War Chief asked another question.

"Oh yes. I like it here," Nick told him.

"The white men at the Great City by the sea of salt said that the boy was stolen," yelled Pocatello. "The father of the boy is getting the army together. The white men are coming to make war on the Shoshone. I say that we should not wait for them to come and shoot all of us with their firesticks. I say we should go to them and burn their houses and their forts. We should kill them and drive all the white men from our land. If the white man wants to have the boy back, I say we should give them his body without its scalp."

"Oh I knew! I Knew!" wailed Old Mother. "You only want to kill my boy!"

"Be still, Grandmother." Old Morogoni spoke with authority. "This boy has been a brave Shoshone. He saved our horses from the Crows. He drove the bear away from our children. He has shown that he is truly one of the Real People. We will not give him to anyone only to have him killed."

"But we do not want a war," said the War Chief. "We lost a large number of our warriors to the Crows. We cannot fight the white man now."

"The white boy's father is coming to attack us. He will hunt us down. He will get the soldiers to fight against us." Pocatello jumped to his feet, shrieking at the council.

That isn't true, thought Nick. Pa would never come to get me. He always told me, "If you ever leave home, don't come back." He doesn't even want me back. But Nick didn't say anything out loud.

"We must be calm," said Morogoni, "Then we can make a good decision."

"We will not fight against the white man unless we are attacked," the War Chief said finally.

"No," said Pocatello. "You are too big a coward to fight against anything!" He got more excited as he talked. "Don't ask us to come and fight for you when the white men come." He waved his hands about, then he pointed at Nick. "I would like to get that trouble-making little devil out in the brush. I would have a white, curly-haired scalp to dance around!" And Pocatello, followed by all his warriors stomped out of the tepee.

"We have decided," the War Chief told Nick, next morning. "We will send some men to talk to your father. They will tell him that you came because you wanted to. He will tell the other white men and they will not make war."

When the War Chief had gone back to his own tepee, Nick sat on a log and thought about home. If Pa, or somebody else didn't want to believe the Indians, they might just shoot them. He thought about Old Mother, crying when he was so sick from the dog-bite. He remembered waiting in the slough for the Crows who didn't come. He thought of Washakie riding among the warriors on the top of the hill during the war with the Crows. Then he thought of his sad-eyed Ma at Grantsville. He had had lots of fun with the Indians. He remembered the little antelope that were slaughtered. He remembered Pocatello and the wagon train. The women and their bloody knives, scalping the already-dead Crow warriors. He knew he didn't want anybody to fight or die because of what he had done.

Nick stood up and went to Washakie. "If I knew the way back to Grantsville, I think I would go back to my Pa and Ma. I don't want to go back to stay, but I want to tell them to not be mad at anybody because I left home. Maybe if they saw that I was all right, they would feel better. Then I would come back again and be an Indian."

Washakie's eyes glistened strangely as he looked at Nick. "If that would be your wish, that is what you shall do." Washakie cleared his throat and turned quickly away.

Nick sat beside the warm pool at the foot of the hills. The valley stretched between him and the Great Salt Lake, which reflected the gold color of the sun, mixed with that odd grey that skirted its edges. Fields of grain stubble surrounded the small clapboard and log shanties dotting the countryside. Nick looked at his image in the pool beside him and tried to scrub off the accumulation of dirt. He ran his fingers through his tangled hair. He didn't think he looked much like a white man, but that didn't really matter anyhow. He wouldn't be staying in civilization long.

His new clothes were the latest Indian fashion. Old Mother, Hanabi, and the other women of the tribe, had worked for a week to make his new leggings and tunic. The clothes were trimmed with the new soft red flannel from Old Mother's bolt of cloth. Her tears had dropped on every stitch she had sewn. Beads of every color banded banded the shoulders and front of his tunic. Fringes hung nearly to his knees. Rolled in an antelope hide and tucked into his pack were a dozen pair of moccasins—enough to last until he returned.

The whole tribe heaped presents on him. He received so many many buffalo robes and elk hides that he could not pile them all on his two ponies. Even Patooli and her mother gave him a beaver hide now that he was leaving.

"Take the little Crow pony that you have been breaking. With it, you will be able to carry all your gifts with you," Washakie told Nick.

Mopi, Boni, and Yagamont gave him a bundle containing so many arrows that he couldn't get them all in his quiver. Nick knew they were the best friends that he had ever had. But the gift that he treasured most was from Raida. She came shyly to the log where he was sitting alone the night before he was to leave. She handed him a bundle, then ducked her head and turned her face away.

Nick spread open the bundle, then gasped. It was the skin full of holes.

"Oh, Raida, you shouldn't give your bear skin away. It is the very first thing you ever tanned. It means too much to you."

"I want you to have it. If you hadn't taken me from the mouth of the giant bear, I would never have been here to tan this little one," Raida told him. "I want you to have it so you won't forget me."

126

"Thank you," he said. His heart bumped against his ribs. "I will keep it until I return. Then I will give it back to you." Nick wished that he hadn't told Buffalo Slayer that he didn't want Raida for his woman. Maybe someday he might want to bring her to live with him and Old Mother, as Washakie had brought Hanabi.

"Oh no! Do not go." Old Mother clung to him and sobbed.

"I will be back," Nick answered her. "I'll be back soon. Don't cry."

That had been last week—before Yagamont's father and Morogoni's son Large Eagle had guided him across the mountains. "You will be in Grantsville in six days," they told him, as they helped him pack his horses this morning. "We will leave you here. You may travel to your white home alone."

"I will be back to our camp in a week or two," said Nick.

"No," said Yegamont's father. "You had better wait until the water runs in the spring. Some of our people will be near. You can find them and they will take you to the old grandmother."

Nick wished that they had come with him a little farther. He got back on his pinto, and leading his two packhorses, he rode down the dusty main street of a little town called Ogden.

Two boys about nine years old dashed at him from a nearby house. One of them threw a small stone, hitting his pinto on the flank. She gave a little bucking hop, dragging the packhorses after her.

"Hey, mister red-assed Injun, get out of our town," the other boy yelled. They spat at him and raced back to the shelter of the house. *I ought to chase them down and pound faces into the ground,* thought Nick.

He remembered what his Ma always said. "Don't pay no mind to those boys, Nicky. Your name is Nicholas. That means 'The People's Victory. Be Victorious.'"

He tapped his pinto across the rump with his lasso and kept on riding toward home.

I would like to thank the descendants of "Uncle Nick" as well as the National Park Service experts of the Pony Express for their invaluable information and inspiration in creating this story and providing details that helped to bring the characters and settings to life.

Anita Twitchell

Further acknowledgements go to Susanne Hülsmann for her amazing help, and to Nina Luijben for the gorgeous work on the cover image.

Jessica Augustsson

About the Author

Anita Twitchell was born Anita Hubbard in Elba, Idaho in 1926, and though she had many an adventure in other places, she returned there upon retirement. Anita was the wife of another Elba native, Charles Twitchell, who was the great-grandson of the sister of Elijah Nicholas Wilson, whose life's story was the seed of inspiration for this book. Anita wrote this story more than twenty years ago, and at the prompting of her daughter and granddaughter, has been persuaded to finally share it with others.

Made in the USA
Las Vegas, NV
30 January 2022